The Gnome's Eye

ANNA KERZ

ORCA BOOK PUBLISHERS

Library and Archives Canada Cataloguing in Publication

Kerz, Anna, 1947-
The gnome's eye / written by Anna Kerz.

ISBN 978-1-55469-195-1

I. Title.
PS8621.E79G56 2010   jC813'.6   C2009-906858-3

First published in the United States, 2010
Library of Congress Control Number: 2009940907

Summary: When Theresa and her family immigrate to Canada after World War II, she confronts her many fears with the help of a talisman given to her by a friend in Austria.

Mixed Sources
Cert no. SW-COC-001271
© 1996 FSC
FSC

Orca Book Publishers is dedicated to preserving the environment and has printed this book on paper certified by the Forest Stewardship Council.

Orca Book Publishers gratefully acknowledges the support for its publishing programs provided by the following agencies: the Government of Canada through the Canada Book Fund and the Canada Council for the Arts, and the Province of British Columbia through the BC Arts Council and the Book Publishing Tax Credit.

Cover artwork by Eric Field
Cover design by Teresa Bubela
Text design and typesetting by Nadja Penaluna
Author photo by Frank Kerz

Orca Book Publishers
PO Box 5626, Stn. B
Victoria, BC Canada
V8R 6S4

Orca Book Publishers
PO Box 468
Custer, WA USA
98240-0468

www.orcabook.com
Printed and bound in Canada.
Printed on 100% PCW recycled paper.
13 12 11 10 • 4 3 2 1

"I'm sorry," I said. "It's just that I don't like to be called 'Mouse.' It's what Tati calls me whenever he thinks I'm afraid."

"He probably doesn't mean it like that."

"Yes, he does!" The words crackled between us. "Well, maybe not…but still…"

I walked on.

"So, what *is* bothering you?"

I sighed. "My oma's coming. She's going to sleep over."

"But that's good news. Omas bring presents."

"Yours, maybe. Not mine. She's the only oma I have left, and I haven't seen her since 1946. I was two. That was eight years ago. She's never come to visit before, and the only presents she sends are meters of cloth for my school dresses."

Martin nodded as if he understood.

"Ha! You *think* you know, but you don't." I looked around to see if anyone might be listening, but of course no one was. There was nothing in the muddy fields on our right except a few patches of snow. "You don't know *my* oma," I said in a low voice. "*My* oma has hair on her teeth!"

Martin's gray eyes widened. "She has hairy teeth?"

I snorted. "Not real hair. It's an expression. My father says it means Oma says whatever she wants and doesn't care who gets hurt when she says it."

One

"...and stay away from the river," my mother called as I stormed out our barrack door.

Too angry to answer, I leaped down the two steps from our stoop and hurried away.

Martin, who had been waiting outside, had to run to catch up. "What's the matter with you, Theresa?" he asked as he trotted along beside me.

"Nothing. I'm going to school, same as you."

"Well, you don't have to be miserable about it. You look like a mouse that fell into a milk pail."

"I'm not a mouse!" I snarled.

Martin ducked and put his hands up as if to protect himself. "I can see that," he said. Then he smiled, and I couldn't help but smile back.

1

*For my parents, who had the courage
to face the unknown.*

"Is that why you're worried?"

I nodded.

"No wonder."

His understanding melted the last of my anger, and my words tumbled out like potatoes from a sack. "She's coming to say goodbye. Because…because we're leaving. We're…migrating?"

"Emigrating?"

"Yes. Emigrating."

"When?"

"That's just it. We're leaving for Canada before the end of the month, and my parents waited till this morning to tell me!"

For once Martin ran out of words, and for the rest of the way to school the only sound we heard came from the snow-swollen river that ran along the left side of our path.

⟿

In the summer our river ran deep and slow, but in the spring, when the snow on the distant mountains melted, it tore through our valley like an express train.

"Stay away from the river" was my mother's final warning every morning before I left for school, and because I was afraid of the water, I obeyed her. But it didn't keep us from stopping at the place where the river curved and watching to see what was being carried along.

That afternoon, as we made our way home again, a small tree came floating toward us. It twisted in the swirling current until, almost directly below where we stood, it crashed into the bank and rose as if it wanted to walk out of the water. Gasping, we jumped back to avoid the branches that reached for us like gnarled, grasping fingers. Then we stared in silence until the river sucked it back and carried it away.

"That was a witch tree," Martin whispered. "It's probably on a journey to find a princess as a sacrifice to calm the river spirits."

Martin had a really good imagination. He could make up stories about anything, and usually, when he started, I joined in. This time I was not in a story-telling mood.

"River spirits?" I scoffed. "There are no river spirits in Austria."

He shrugged. "There aren't any princesses either. So why can't we sacrifice a pretend princess to pretend spirits?"

"Fine! Do whatever you want," I said, and I stalked away.

Of course I expected Martin to catch up. But he didn't, and when I looked back, the path behind me was empty. A fist of worry formed in my chest.

When I retraced my steps, I found him down beside the river, hopping from one spray-spattered rock to the next. Every time he moved, he stopped and peered at the ground. Finally he bent, scooped up a stone and clambered back up to the road.

"Are you crazy?" I yelled as soon as he was safely on the path.

"Probably." He grinned, showing off the gap between his teeth.

"Doesn't *your* mother tell you to stay away from the water?"

He shook his head. "Mostly she throws up her hands and says, 'Talking to you is a waste of my breath.'"

He held out a small, round white stone. "Here," he said. "It's for you. It's a gnome's eye. You can tell by its size and the color."

"It's a river stone. You could have fallen into the water for a river stone!" I was shouting, but Martin didn't seem to notice.

"A gnome's eye always turns to stone when it falls out," he said, and I knew he wasn't going to let this story go. There was nothing to do but walk away or join in.

I sighed. "A gnome lost his eye?" I said more quietly.

"Probably another gnome found his treasure… and…and they fought, and…and one of them died. Their eyes always fall out when they die."

"What happened to the other eye?"

He shrugged. "Maybe it got lost. Or maybe his family has it…they would have come for his body… they would have carried him home. Maybe they took it along." He held out the stone again. "Here. Take it."

"Uh-uh!" I put my hands behind my back. I didn't want to touch a gnome's eye, even if it did look like a stone.

"A gnome's eye is just what you need if you're leaving," he said. "No matter where you go, it will keep you safe. It will protect you from all things evil, alive or dead. Take it."

What can it hurt? I thought. I reached out, but when our hands came close, a spark flashed between us and we both pulled back.

"See?" Martin said. "Magic."

"Or static electricity." I laughed, but when he held the stone toward me again, I refused it, and it was Martin who slipped it into his coat pocket.

He didn't say anything else until we reached the entrance to our lager. "I know you don't want to go," he said, "but look at what you're leaving."

His words surprised me. I knew how Lager Lichtenstein looked. Our unpainted barracks were ages old and grayed by the weather. They were surrounded by kitchen gardens, tangles of laundry lines, sagging chicken coops and pigpens held together with rusted nails and baling wire. Not even the beauty of the distant mountains improved its appearance.

I thought of the sly looks people gave us when they heard where we lived. "Refugees," they called us when they were being polite. Sometimes, when they thought we couldn't hear, they whispered other words.

In spite of all that, the lager was the only home I knew, and the thought of leaving made my stomach clench.

The wind picked up. I didn't mind, because I was wearing the coat Tati had made over from Mami's old one. It was brown and fuzzy, with an extra lining that made it especially warm. There was nothing warm about Martin's coat. It was a gray tweed, old and worn thin. A man's coat too wide for his narrow shoulders. I saw him shiver.

"They say it's always cold in Canada," he teased as he turtled his head into his scarf.

"Then it's a good thing you're not going," I said. "You'd freeze."

"Ha! You're probably right," he said. "Just you be careful when you get there so those Canadians don't mistake you for a bear. You don't want to end up as a rug on somebody's living-room floor."

I rolled my eyes and Martin laughed before he turned and ran for home.

Two

For the next two days, Mami got ready for Oma's visit by washing and cleaning every corner of our two small rooms. I thought it was silly, all that work, when we were leaving anyway. I didn't like that it made her grumpy and that nothing I did was good enough.

"Stay out of my way," she snapped every time I tried to help. That made me grumpy too.

And then she cooked one of my least favorite meals. Sausages with sauerkraut. I didn't mind the sausage, but the sauerkraut...?

"Eat," Mami scolded as I sat staring at the soggy mass steaming on my plate. "Eat! You're nothing but skin and bones. What will your oma think? She'll take one look and say you're a walking skeleton."

I huffed, pretending I didn't care what my oma might think, but the image of a walking skeleton, bones clacking, began to fill my head. The picture was not a pretty one. Neither was the smell of the sauerkraut. I sat staring at my plate until Mami yelled, "*Herr Yemmini!*" I didn't know what her words meant, but I knew she only said them when she was really mad. When she pulled the wooden spoon from the drawer and whacked it on the table, I flinched. I knew how much that spoon hurt when it was whacked against my bottom. Even so, I was determined not to eat, so I ignored the warnings and let our clock *tick-tock* the minutes away.

Ten minutes later it was Mami who gave in. "You're impossible," she sputtered. "Go and kneel!" So I went to my punishment corner by the door. Kneeling made my knees hurt, but even that was better than eating sauerkraut.

That night my mother's warnings invaded my dreams. I saw the flesh fall from my body until there was nothing left except my organs: my heart, my liver and my stomach, all bunched up inside the cage of my rib bones.

"Didn't I tell you this would happen?" Mami wailed. "Oh, why didn't you eat?"

"I'll eat," I promised, beginning to sob. But when an enormous plate of sauerkraut appeared, I gagged and began to cough. With each cough, bits of me jiggled loose. I grabbed for my belly to hold everything in, but my intestines slipped between my bony fingers and fell to the floor like a heap of linked sausages.

"We'll put them in the smokehouse with the hams," I heard Tati say.

"Nooo!" I screamed. "Nooo! Don't hang me with the hams."

I was shouting and flailing when the bedroom light flashed on and Mami's hands shook me awake. "Theresa!" she whispered. "Theresa! Hush!"

I gasped and sat up, relieved to see skin covering my bones, relieved to find my mother by my bed and my father beside the light switch.

"What's the matter, Mouse?" he asked.

As I sobbed out my story, Mami crossed herself. "It's all that reading you do," she said. "You've ended up with too much imagination."

But Tati, who hated tears, raked his fingers through his auburn hair, as he always did when he was annoyed. "This is your fault too, Leni," he scolded my mother. "It's all your fussing and worrying. No wonder she has such dreams."

His words made Mami cry, and when I saw the first tear streak down her cheek, I cried louder.

"Oh, for goodness sake!" Tati groaned. "You two will have everybody in this barrack awake. Lie down and be quiet. Both of you." He switched off the light and groped his way back to bed while I did my best to swallow my tears.

In the darkness I felt Mami's hands straighten my bed coverings. She leaned down, touched her damp cheek to my forehead as if she was checking my temperature, then stepped away. I heard their straw-filled mattress rustle as she lay down beside my father. Soon I could tell from the sounds of their breathing that they were asleep.

I wished I could sleep.

It started to rain, the first drops sounding like little *pings* and *tings* on the roof. Lightning flashed. There was a distant rumble of thunder. I groaned and slipped deeper into the warmth of my duvet. Daytime thunderstorms were exciting. Night storms were a different story. I wished I was small enough to slip across into my parents' bed; the storm didn't seem to be bothering them.

More rain fell. I began to think about Oma's visit.

I didn't know much about Oma, except that she lived a train ride away in a different lager, near the city of Rottenmann. And I knew she never came to visit. Once or twice a year Mami went there, but she always went alone. "It costs too much for all of us to go," she'd say. Or, "There's no place for you to sleep in Oma's small room."

I didn't complain. In our pictures Oma looked bent and old, more like the witch in Hansel and Gretel than the smiling, huggy Oma I wished for. Still, I used to wonder why we never saw her. But when I found out last summer, I wasn't any happier.

Mami and our neighbor, Frau Besselmeyer, had been making jam. They were in our kitchen, taking turns stirring to keep the fruit from sticking to the bottom of the pot. When it thickened, loud *Blub! Blub! Blub!* sounds erupted from the mixture and, with each bubble a searing splatter of jam spurted out.

"Go," Mami told me as she wrapped a rag around her arm to protect it from the scalding jam. "I have enough to think about without worrying about you. Get right out of the kitchen."

It was Frau Besselmeyer who helped me carry a chair outside. I sat sewing a cross-stitch pattern along the edge of a handkerchief. Waves of overheated air wafted from the window above me, carrying the tangy aroma of the cooking damson plums and the voices of Mami and Frau Besselmeyer. I didn't pay much attention to what they were saying, until I heard Mami say, "My mother warned me not to marry Adam." Then I really started to listen.

"It was because he has red hair," Mami went on. "It was something about Judas and Cain in the Bible, and how they both had red hair."

"A lot of the old people believed that," Frau Besselmeyer said. "They thought that people with red hair were not to be trusted. It was a foolish belief."

"Yes," Mami agreed. "Very foolish. But I couldn't convince my mother of that. 'You'll be cursed if you marry him,' she said. Luckily my father was a sensible man. When he gave us his blessing, we married anyway."

"So things worked out in the end?"

"Not really. After the wedding we had to live in their house, and my mother blamed Adam's hair for everything that went wrong. She didn't say anything to him of course, but I heard plenty. She even blamed his hair when the chickens stopped laying eggs!

"And then the war started, and didn't she blame that on his hair too! 'See,' she told me. 'See what curses you've brought down on us.' I think she was relieved when the men were called to the army and Adam left."

"It must have been a difficult time for you," Frau Besselmeyer said.

"It wasn't easy. And it only got harder when Adam came home on leave and I got pregnant."

"That should have made your mother happy."

"Ha! You might think so. But for nine months I heard: 'Only a red-headed man would want to bring a child into the world in the middle of a war!' Then Theresa was born. When my mother saw her hair, she made an enormous fuss.

" 'The child has red hair! Red hair! Nobody in *our* family has red hair. I told you not to marry that man. Now look what you've got. *A gashtiches Kind! So a gashtiches Kind!* An ugly child. Such an ugly child!' "

Frau Besselmeyer made sympathetic noises with her tongue, but my stomach clenched. My oma thinks I'm ugly?

"She'll change her mind when she sees Theresa this time," Frau Besselmeyer hurried to say. "Her red hair is beautiful—and all those curls!"

I heard, but her words did nothing to soften the sting of "Such an ugly child!" And it was no comfort to hear Mami say, "I doubt my mother will ever change."

I thought about walking away from the window to keep from hearing more, but before I could move, Mami went on. "We were already here, in Austria, all of us living in the barrack in Rottenmann when my father died. My mother was beside herself. She blamed Adam's hair for that too. When he heard, Adam was furious. 'The war was bad enough,' he shouted. 'I had to come home to this?'

"There was a lot of shouting, and the next day Adam got permission to move us here. We left, and my mother has never come to visit."

Now, lying awake in the middle of the night, I remembered Mami's words. She's coming now, I thought. And a twist of worry tightened in my chest.

Outside, it started to rain. Thunder made the window rattle and our wooden walls vibrate.

"Mami?" I whispered into the darkness.

"Hmmm?"

"I'm scared."

She didn't say anything, but she slipped out of her bed and into mine. Her arm pulled me close, and I curled into her warmth. I might have slept then, but from the other side of the plank wall, Herr Besselmeyer began to cough. The sound was wet and harsh, as if it was being ripped from his chest.

Tati groaned but didn't say a word of complaint. We all knew how much the coughing pained Herr Besselmeyer, and we knew how embarrassed he was because his coughs disturbed the night for all six families in our barrack.

As the rain fell, Herr Besselmeyer coughed on and on. By the time he stopped, the rain had let up too. Tati sighed and turned over. In the silence we heard a loud, rumbling fart, followed by Herr Besselmeyer's grumbly voice. "Sorry," he said.

I giggled until Mami said, "Hush!" After a while I slept, but in my dreams Oma followed me around carrying a platter piled high with steaming sauerkraut.

Three

My mother insisted that we walk to the station together. I didn't want to go. "Why do I have to? I'll see Oma when she get's here," I said.

Tati was putting on his best white shirt. The one Mami had boiled and starched. I could hear the fabric crackle as he pushed his arms into the sleeves. "We all have to face what we can't avoid," he said, fastening the buttons. "Besides, why should I suffer alone?"

"Don't start!" Mami warned.

He winked, and I stopped complaining, but all the way to the station I dragged my feet through the dirt at the side of the road.

"Look at your shoes!" Mami scolded when she noticed. "What will your oma think?"

I looked. The bright shine I had polished into my shoes that morning was buried under a fine layer of road dust. It gave me a kind of satisfaction. There, I thought. Now Oma won't think that I went to any trouble to impress her.

The train was rolling to a stop as we arrived. Brakes squealed. The engine hissed out clouds of steam that billowed along the platform. It made the arriving passengers look as if they were stepping out of a roiling fog.

Mami walked toward an old woman. As they linked arms and turned toward us, Tati stepped forward and reached for the woman's suitcase. She wouldn't let go. She spread her legs and clutched the handle with both hands, making Tati look like a thief trying to wrench it from her. His face flushed, and he stepped back. The woman held the case. Tati frowned.

This was Oma? Yes. It had to be. She was smaller than I had expected, dwarfed by the black woolen shawl that hung from her shoulders and the dark skirts that swirled around her ankles. Her face looked thin and gray in the shadow of her kerchief.

Say something, I told myself when she stopped in front of me. Say something. I knew I should curtsy. I should put out my hand. I should say *Grüss Gott*, because that was the polite way to say hello. I should say something, but I couldn't think what, because Oma's needle-sharp eyes were examining my hair, my clothes, my dust-covered shoes.

"Glasses?" she said, turning to Mami. "Now she needs glasses?" She shook her head. "The child is downright homely."

My heart fell to my feet. She still thinks I'm ugly, I thought, but before I could think of what to say or do, Oma yanked me forward, wrapped her wiry arms around me and clutched me to her bony chest.

That evening we had a big dinner. There was soup, full of Mami's homemade noodles, an oven-roasted chicken and potatoes, followed by slices of strudel, thick with poppy seeds and rich with raisins.

Oma didn't eat much. She tasted everything, but finished nothing.

"We killed the last hen for you," I said, my voice shrill. I knew how much work had gone into making the meal.

"The last hen, for the last meal," Oma said. Nobody spoke after that.

Right after dinner Mami and Oma pulled their chairs to the stove and sat, whispering. Tati left, making excuses about a neighbor's coat that needed to be measured. I stayed at the table, washing the dinner dishes in the dishpan. By the time Tati came back, the fire had burned down and the kitchen was cooling. There was nothing left to do but go to bed.

We were already in our nightclothes when Oma said, "Adam, bring me my suitcase."

Tati fetched the case he hadn't been allowed to hold in the station, and Oma's gnarled fingers unlatched the clasps and lifted the lid. She pulled out a small, flat package wrapped in brown paper. "Give me your hand, Theresa," she said.

When I gave her my right hand, she placed the package into my palm.

Mami nodded, so I folded back the paper. Inside was a pair of gold earrings.

"They're for you," Oma said. She cleared her throat. "Your ota gave them to me on our wedding day."

I stared at the unexpected gift, and for one long moment I regretted all my wicked thoughts. Gold earrings. I held them out for Mami and Tati to see. They glowed, reflecting the ceiling light. Into that warm silence Oma said, "You never know. Sometimes even homely girls find men who want to marry them. Take care of the earrings, and you'll have something nice to wear on your wedding day."

Tati sputtered and turned away to cough.

"Say 'thank you,' Theresa," Mami hurried to say.

"Thank you," I said, but the earrings had lost their glow.

Oma reached into her suitcase again to lift out a large bedsheet. "This," she said, handing the sheet to my mother, "is made from the flax that grew in our fields at home. My grandmother made it for my trousseau. I watched her spin the thread and weave it on her loom. Everything else was left behind when we left Yugoslavia. You might as well take it if you're going to this new life in America. I don't have anything else to give you."

Mami's eyes were moist with tears as she kissed Oma's cheek. "Thank you," she began.

"Don't thank me," Oma snapped. "I've had it for fifty years, and it's good as new. I'll be happy if you can do half as well."

"And you," she went on, frowning at Tati. "You take care. If you must drag them to the far corners of the Earth, you'd better watch out. I'll haunt you forever if anything happens to them!"

"I don't doubt that at all," Tati said with a grin.

Mami poked her elbow into his side, but his grin stayed. I don't think Oma noticed, because she was busy pulling a gray ribbon from inside the waistband of her skirt. On the end of the ribbon was a small cloth bag, and when that was open, she shook out a handful of coins.

"Take them," she said, thrusting them at Tati. "I've been saving."

"You don't have to…," he began.

"Take it!" she said. "And be careful. You never know what kind of thieves and robbers live in foreign places."

Tati glanced at the money and then at my mother. I saw her nod again, and he bowed, as if Oma was a grand lady, before he slipped the money into his pocket.

"Hmmmph!" Oma said, but she looked pleased. Then she pulled out one last gift and handed it to Mami. "This one is for all of you. To remember me," she said. It was a photograph. In it, Oma's dark eyes glared out from under a black kerchief.

Mami took it and held it to her chest.

"You should go to sleep now," Oma said. "I'm tired."

That night Oma shared my bed. We were both skinny, but she seemed to take up a lot of room. She was cold and hard, with sharp bony edges. And she farted. Not as loud as Herr Besselmeyer, but loud enough. And her farts didn't make me giggle.

In the morning, when I woke, she was still beside me, whispering with Mami.

"I'll die alone," I heard her say. "I'll die alone." She cried then, and when Mami cried too, a huge wave of pity washed over me: for Oma, for Mami, for me. Why should we leave if the leaving hurts? I wondered.

"I think we should stay," I said, sitting up. "That way Oma won't have to die alone."

I thought my words would make her happy, but Oma bolted up in bed.

"*Du?*" she said, glaring at me. "*Du?* What makes you think you have something to say?"

Then she whirled and, waving a warning finger at Mami, she said, "*Kinderwille ist Hingelsdreck!* The wants of children are as worthless as chicken droppings!"

"Now stop fussing and do what your mother tells you," she finished more quietly.

We got up then and had breakfast.

In the afternoon we walked Oma back to the station and watched as she boarded her train.

"*Auf Wiedersehen! Auf Wiedersehen!*" we called as the train pulled away.

"Will she come to Canada when we get there?" I asked.

Tati made a rumbling sound deep in his throat, and Mami wiped away tears, but nobody answered my question.

Four

On Saturday morning Mami and I settled beside the kitchen stove to knit. I was making a square, or trying to. It was not what I wanted to make. I wanted to make something real, like a scarf or a hat, but Mami said, "If you can't knit a square, you can't knit." This was my third try, and it was not going well. Every time I wrapped the yarn around one needle, it was a struggle to slip it to the next.

"You're strangling your stitches," Mami warned.

I sighed and loosened my grip, but as soon as I did, a stitch escaped and others followed.

"Aghhh!" I groaned, yanking on the yarn. And just like that, a whole row of knitting unraveled. Fine! I thought, pulling the rest apart too.

My mother's needles clicked on. "We'll have to pack carefully," she said, as if she hadn't noticed what I was doing. "There's not much room in the trunk. We can only take things that can't be replaced, like our duvet. We have to take that. That duvet is filled with the feathers of generations of geese from home, and I knew each and every one of those birds!"

Her needles stopped, and she allowed her knitting to settle on her lap. "I wish you could have seen them," she said as I rewound my yarn. "Every spring your oma sat on a stool in the yard behind the kitchen clutching one goose after the other between her knees. She pulled only the softest, downiest feathers from the breast."

"That must have hurt," I said.

"Oh, no. You know how loose feathers are in the spring. Birds pull them out to line their nests." She laughed. "They were so raggedy once their feathers were gone. They stretched their necks and tried to look dignified, but stray fluff stuck out at all angles, and patches of pink goose flesh showed through. They were about as elegant as a beggar woman dressed in a ball gown from a refuse bin."

Her smiled faded as she picked up her work and began recounting stitches. "I'm not leaving it," she said when she was done. "It's coming with us!"

"We'll never be able to replace my sled either," I said, expecting Mami to say, "Of course not," but she shook her head. "We can't take that," she said. "It's far too big."

I was ready to argue, but our talk was interrupted by three sharp raps on the wall. "Frau Besselmeyer needs me," I said, happy to leave my knitting behind.

"Go then," Mami said.

I didn't wait to be told a second time. For as long as I could remember, the Besselmeyers had lived beside us in a room that was both bedroom and kitchen. They were an older couple with no children of their own. Mami said they spoiled me, but I didn't mind being spoiled.

Every so often Frau Besselmeyer knocked and asked a favor.

"I need some flour," she might say. Or she might ask for sugar, or a loaf of bread, and I would run to the lager store for her. But mostly when she knocked, it was because she was finished mixing a cake and needed someone to lick the empty bowl, or because she had some extra raisins that might dry out if they weren't eaten.

Frau Besselmeyer opened her door just far enough to let me slip inside.

"Watch where you're stepping," Herr Besselmeyer warned from his chair by the stove as a whole brood of downy chicks came chirping and cheeping across the room.

"Ohh!" I said, picking up one of the tiny yellow birds. "They're so small."

"Not for long," Herr Besselmeyer said.

I nodded. Most years Mami kept poultry too, so I knew how quickly chickens grew. It would only be days before they sprouted feathers. Then they'd be moved to the henhouse, where they'd stay as long as they could lay eggs. Once they stopped laying, they'd go into a pot for Sunday dinner.

"We're not getting chicks this year," I said, pleased that I had news to share. "Or piglets. Tati says there's no point. We won't be here to see them grow."

Frau Besselmeyer turned away.

"I have to leave everything behind," I went on, happy to have someone who would listen to my troubles. "Mami's taking our duvet, but she says I can't bring my sled."

Frau Besselmeyer sniffed and blew her nose. The sound caught my attention. "Oh. Oh," I said when I saw her tears.

Tears blurred my eyes too, as Frau Besselmeyer's stout arms reached out and pulled me close. "You could come," I said, my face pressed to her chest. "You could get papers and come to Canada too."

Frau Besselmeyer didn't answer, or if she did, I didn't hear because Herr Besselmeyer started coughing.

"It's the draft," she said. "It followed you in.

Any little draft makes him cough."

When he was done, Frau Besselmeyer picked up a blanket-wrapped bundle from the bed. "For you," she said, placing it in my arms. "To remember us."

In the bundle was a doll. I stared at it, not sure what to say. A doll? I was too old for dolls. Still, this wasn't a cloth-and-rag doll like the one Mami made for me when I was small. This was a store-bought baby doll with fisted hands and sleepy eyes. And it was big. Every bit as big as a real baby. And the hair painted on its head was red. Red, like mine. Maybe I wasn't too big for this doll. Maybe it was meant to be mine.

"She's…beautiful!" I said. And then I groaned.

"You don't like it?" Herr Besselmeyer sounded worried.

"I do," I said, cradling the baby. "But it's so big. What if Mami says I have to leave it behind?"

"She'll make room for her," Frau Besselmeyer said. "I promise."

She was right, of course. Mami thought the doll was beautiful. "What will you name her?" she asked.

"Lissi, I think. Because Lissi is Frau Besselmeyer's first name. And I'll carry her all the way," I added, thinking about space in the trunk.

But Mami surprised me again. "Lissi will be safer packed away," she said, and she wouldn't change her mind, no matter how much I pleaded.

Five

One by one our belongings were sorted into piles: things to take, things to sell, things to give away.

I was mad all over again when I saw my sled in the giveaway pile.

"Why does it have to stay? It was always the smallest sled on the hill."

"It's small for a sled, but it's too big for the trunk," Mami said.

Annoyed, I picked it up and stomped across to Martin's barrack. "Here," I said, thrusting my sled into his arms. "You can have it."

He held it to his chest. "Thank you," he said, but he didn't look happy.

"What's the matter? All winter you complained

I didn't let you have enough turns. Now you don't want it?"

"I want it."

"Well then?"

"Sliding down the hills won't be as much fun without you. Who will I argue with?"

"I have to give up my sled, and you make jokes?" I turned and stomped back home.

When I walked into the kitchen, Mami was leaning over the table, where she had spread our photographs.

"That was the house where you were born," she said, picking up a small black-and-white snapshot.

I was still mad about the sled, so I didn't say anything, but Mami went on.

"Your ota built it. You can't tell from this, but the shutters were green, and every summer the window boxes were filled with red geraniums. The walls were painted white, and they were so thick that the house was always warm in winter, and cool even in the hot days of summer."

I sighed. It was hard to resist a story. "Why did we leave?" I asked.

"There's no simple answer to that," she said. "You have to go back all the way to a time when the king of the Austro-Hungarian Empire sent people down the Danube River to settle the land."

"But where did they come from?"

"I think our ancestors came from Germany, but others came from Austria, France, Switzerland. They were mostly young people, sent with tools and seeds and household items. When they arrived, they found a wild, swampy land that was nowhere near ready for farming."

"Didn't they want to go back home?"

"Of course. But in life you make choices, and then you're stuck with them. They had to stay, even when people started to die of fevers or starvation."

"They didn't bring food?"

"They did, but it was a long time before they could grow new crops."

She sighed. "Anyway, all that happened almost two hundred years ago. In the meantime, the king died and his empire was divided up into different countries. They called the part where our people lived Yugoslavia, and they called us Danube Swabians because we came down the Danube River on barges that set out from a part of Germany called Swabia."

"If we came from Germany, how come we aren't German now?"

"We have German roots, and our language is German, but after so many years we're not German citizens anymore."

"Were we happy? In Yugoslavia, I mean."

"We were. We had our houses and farms, and we got along with our neighbors. Then the Second World War started."

"That was a bad time."

"Wars always are. Everyone is called to fight. Our men had a choice. They could join the German or the Hungarian army, and because we spoke German, most of them signed up to fight for Germany."

"And Germany lost the war."

"They did."

"So why did we come here?"

"In 1944, when the war was coming to an end, the Russian army was moving closer to our towns. They threatened to take over. We had no choice. We could stay and become Communists or go. So we packed our wagons with whatever we could carry, and we left."

"And we walked all the way to Austra," I said, helping the story along.

"Yes, all the way."

"It was a long way."

"A very long way."

"Did *we* have food?"

"Some, but not enough. I was sick with worry because you were so small. Not even a year old. In some ways that was good, because I was still nursing, so you had something to eat. But we had to keep stopping to buy or beg for more." She gave a small, dry laugh. "We stopped at every place that stank."

"You stopped at stinky places?" I wrinkled my nose.

"Think about it. Farm animals make smells. Places that didn't have smells didn't have food."

I nodded. It made sense. "Were you scared?"

"Every day. For you, for me, for all the children and old people walking with us. And when we got here, they called us refugees. When we spoke, they laughed and pretended not to understand. 'You're Danube Swabians?' they said. 'It's time you learned to speak German properly.' And we realized we sounded different. Old-fashioned."

"Did anybody stay behind?"

"Some people did. Your Aunt Theresa, she stayed." Mami handed me another photograph. "That's her, beside her husband, and their two children. The picture was taken before the war, when the family was still together. Then your uncle went off to fight with all the other soldiers, but he never came back. When we packed to leave, Theresa wanted to go, but her father-in-law was old and too sick to travel.

"'I'm the only family he has left,' she said. 'I can't walk away and leave him. The children and I will stay.' And she did."

"What happened to them?"

"Her father-in-law didn't last long. There were no doctors and no medicine. He died. And after the war, Theresa and the children were put into a labor camp. She died there. Starved or froze or died of disease. We never found out."

"That happened *after* the war?"

Mami pulled a handkerchief from her apron pocket and blew her nose. "Wars end," she said. "Papers are signed. Soldiers are sent home, but the pain and anger people feel…sometimes it lasts for years and years."

"What happened to my cousins?"

"During the war, things were hard, but *after* the war, things were harder. There was no food. People didn't have medicine or clothes to wear. There was nothing. Children without family…they had no chance."

"You mean they died?"

She shrugged. "We don't know. We tried to find out through the Red Cross, but thousands of people were moved from one country to the next. People who were shipped into Russia just disappeared."

I stared at the picture of my Aunt Theresa—the aunt who gave me her name—standing beside her family.

"It's not fair," I said.

"No," Mami agreed. "Life isn't."

There was a sadness in her voice that brought tears to my eyes. Compared to what my family had left behind, my sled was nothing.

Six

O n our last day in the lager, Martin and I walked home from school together. We stopped at the river's curve and watched the water tumble over the stones. I wanted to see and remember everything in case I never came back. Martin shifted from foot to foot. "What's the matter? Are you bored?" I asked.

He looked embarrassed. "I have a present for you," he said, thrusting a small bundle of postcards at me. "They're so you can write. That way I'll know all about the voyage, and what there is in Canada. In case I get a chance to go."

"Oh," I said. "Thank you."

"You know," he went on in a low voice, "when you sail, there are things you have to watch out for."

"What? What do I have to watch out for?"

"Well, rats. Watch out for rats. If you see them leave the ship, you'll know it's going down."

"What do you mean going down?"

"You know. To the bottom of the sea."

"Do you think I want to hear that now?"

"It's so you'll know what to do if something happens."

"Nothing's going to happen!"

"You never know. The *Titanic* hit an iceberg. Everybody said it would never, ever sink, but it did. And it was new."

"What happened to the people?"

"The ones in the lifeboats were rescued. A lot drowned."

"And the rats?"

"I don't know. People don't talk about rat survivors."

"I...I can't swim."

"Doesn't matter. The water's too cold for that anyway. Especially now. It's full of icebergs in the spring. Just remember to get to a lifeboat. Push your way to the front of the line if you have to, but make sure you get a seat. And dress warm. The winds on the North Atlantic are freezing cold."

I cringed at the image of a lifeboat drifting through a sea of ice.

"And there's something else you should remember. When you get thirsty, don't drink the ocean water. It's full of salt, and that will kill you. If you have to drink something, drink your pee."

"Ewww!" I flapped my hands in disgust.

He laughed. I turned to go, but Martin reached for my arm and stopped me. "I want to give you something else," he said.

"You gave me the postcards."

"I know, but the postcards are really for me. This is for you." He held out the gnome's eye. I felt my face flush at the sight of the white stone.

"Take it," he said. "It will protect you from everything."

"That's silly."

"What if it isn't? What if it's true?"

"But it's not."

"Doesn't really matter. Keep it as a souvenir," he said. When I didn't object, he slipped the stone into my pocket.

We walked the rest of the way home side by side, my mind filled with ships and rats and icebergs. Then, just before we separated to go to our own barrack, Martin said, "Oh, and just so you know, when I come to Canada, I'll bring the sled, and if you ask me, I might let you have some turns on the hills."

I snorted, and he laughed. Then we both laughed and said goodbye. But that night when I was in bed, I thought about Martin: about his gap-toothed smile, about his silly stories, about how he teased and how he listened, and I realized I'd miss him more than the sled, more than anything.

The sky was still black when Mami, Tati and I filed out of our barrack the next morning. We had said our goodbyes the night before, so we left as quietly as we could, trying not to wake anyone.

Outside we paused. In the distance lay the low, bulky shapes of the mountains. Around us, rows of silent barracks. Then, from the back of the lager came the sound of a rooster crowing, long and loud. Frau Besselmeyer's bird, I thought. She always said his voice carried as far as the bells on Easter morning.

The rooster's challenge was answered from farmyards across the valley. It made me sad to hear them, because I knew all those birds would crow tomorrow, and the next day, and the day after that, but I wouldn't hear them.

Tati picked up my suitcase in one hand, and his own in the other, and started off. We followed,

Mami and me, all the way to the station. And all the way there, my hand stayed in my pocket, my fingers curled around the stone nestled there. It's only a river stone, I told myself. It has no magic. But there was something about the feel of it in my palm that gave me hope.

Seven

It took two days of traveling by train to get to the ship that would take us to Canada. Two bum-numbing days seated on wooden benches. Two long, boring days as the train *clickity-clacked* past fields, through tunnels, in and out of towns, out of Austria and through Germany. We rolled on until we reached the coastal city of Bremerhaven, where our ship was bobbing in the water beside the dock.

I was surprised at how small it was. And how old. There were streaks of rust bleeding from under the last coat of paint.

It's good that it's old, I told myself. That means it's been across the ocean so often it probably knows the way by heart.

Around us, people stood waiting, tagged and labeled like luggage. I stood between Mami and Tati, letting their bodies protect me from the bite of the wind that blew in from the sea. Every so often a horn blasted out waves of sound that made everybody jump, then laugh nervously before they settled again.

"Men and boys over here," a sailor finally shouted. Tati picked up his suitcase. He turned and nodded at us before he joined the line that wormed its way aboard the ship.

"Tati, wait!" I called, but he didn't look back. "Where is he going?" I asked. "He's not going without us, is he?"

"I don't know," Mami said.

"Don't know…?"

She must have heard the fear in my voice, because she pulled me close. "Of course he's not going without us," she said.

A tall woman with a know-it-all voice spoke up. "The beds for the men are in the front of the ship. Women and children sleep in the middle, where it's not so rough."

"Why can't we sleep in the front with Tati? It doesn't look rough," I said, looking at the wavelets in the harbor.

The woman crossed her arms over her flat chest and stared at me with bulging green eyes. "It soon will be," she said. "My brother works on the docks, and he told me that this old tub has no stabilizers."

"What are stabilizers?"

"You'll find out soon enough," she said, and she smiled a tight, satisfied smile. "You'll find out when we're at sea and everybody's carrying on like a pig on butchering day."

"There's no need to frighten her," Mami said.

"She might as well know what she's in for."

Mami gave my shoulders a reassuring squeeze. "We'll be fine," she said.

I nodded. I so wanted to believe her. I knew what pigs sounded like on butchering day, and I was determined to never sound like that.

Finally a sailor called for women and children to board, and Mami picked up our suitcases. "Stay right behind me," she said as we started up a different gangplank. And I did. I followed so closely that when she stepped through the doorway and stopped, I bumped into her.

"*Mein Gott!*" I heard her say. "We're going right into the mouth of hell."

The mouth of hell? I stretched, anxious to see the mouth of hell for myself, but behind us the know-it-all woman barked, "Move on. Move on. We've been standing long enough." So we scrambled down the steep metal staircase, and it wasn't until we reached the bottom that I was able to see my mother's idea of hell.

There were no flames, just a forest of gun-metal gray bunk beds that filled the belly of the ship. They were set up in groups of four, one upper and lower bunk right beside another upper and lower bunk, the pair separated by a white sheet.

The funny thing was, what Mami thought was "the mouth of hell" made my heart do a little flip. I liked the idea of sleeping in a bunk, and when a sailor directed us to beds that matched the numbers on our tags, I was even more pleased, because I was assigned to sleep on the top, right above my mother.

Gradually, women and children filled the beds around us. Another mother and a small boy settled into the bunks on the other side of our sheet. Ahead of us was a woman with a crying baby. The know-it-all woman was in the bed behind. She was telling anybody who would listen about the missing stabilizers, and she pointed out the small metal boxes welded to our beds.

"The extra cardboard liners are on the shelf by the door," she said. "I asked the sailor when we came in. Heaven knows we'll need them."

Once everybody was settled, we were called for a lifeboat drill, and I was relieved to see that Tati was assigned to our boat.

When the drill was over, we went to the dining room for dinner. Tati told us about his room, and it sounded just like ours, only it was filled with older boys and men. By the time we finished eating, the sun had set, and people drifted off to get ready for bed.

I was in line beside Mami at the row of sinks, waiting for a turn to wash my hands and face and to brush my teeth, when I remembered Martin's rats. There was no sign of them. Not one. I looked behind the doors and under the metal staircases. I checked around the toilet stalls and peered into dark corners. I found rust and dust and things I was afraid to examine, but no rats.

"*What* are you doing?" Mami asked when she saw me on my hands and knees, checking the space under our bunk.

"What?" I sat back on my heels and stared up at her. Her hazel eyes were dark-rimmed, her face worry-lined. What could I tell her? That I was under her bunk looking for rats? "Nothing," I said.

She sighed. "Go to sleep, Theresa," she said.

So I stepped on the metal frame of her bunk and hoisted myself up. My weight made the bedsprings squeal and the mattress sag.

"Lie still up there!" Mami called out. "I don't want you to come down on me."

Shifting more carefully, I settled back and discovered that when I rested my head on my pillow I could see right out the porthole beside my bed. For a while I watched white gulls drifting across the purple sky and small boats beetling between the huge ships that lined the harbor. I felt lucky. My own window. I'd be able to see the whole voyage from my bed.

When it got too dark outside to see anything, I examined the network of pipes and wires crisscrossing the ceiling. A perfect highway for rats, I thought. Then I groaned. Thanks to Martin, I had rats in my brain.

The harbor waves made the *Beaverbrae* rock gently, gently, gently, and eventually I slept. I slept so soundly I didn't hear the sailors seal our windows with steel shutters.

Eight

The engines were pounding when I woke. *Thud-THUD, Thud-THUD, Thud-THUD.* The lights that had glared into my face the night before were dimmed, and everything looked faded somehow, and wrong. Wrong because I knew I was lying in bed, but I could see my toes, and they were higher than my head.

I grabbed for the mattress, afraid I might slide out of bed headfirst. The ship tilted in the opposite direction, and my feet sank as my head lifted. Everything leveled then, but as it did, we rolled from side to side before we began another climb. The motions repeated themselves: a sharp climb, a sudden drop and a wallow. Climb, drop, wallow; climb, drop, wallow.

I turned to the porthole to see what was happening outside, but all I could see was the shadow of my frightened face staring back from the darkened glass.

"Who closed the shutters?" I asked, hoisting myself to my elbow.

Mistake. As I rose, my stomach rose too, and something in my belly clenched. There was just enough time to stretch toward my barf box before my stomach heaved, and I threw up. The clenching happened again, and again, and again. My stomach emptied, but even when nothing else came up, the heaving went on, sending arrows of pain through my middle. It was a long time before I sagged to my mattress, whimpering.

"Mami?" I called. No answer.

The climb and drop and wallow continued. I must have slept again, but when I woke, I didn't feel any better.

"Mami?" I called again.

Still no answer. Carefully, so I wouldn't jiggle my stomach, I shifted to the edge of the bed and leaned down to peer into my mother's bunk. She was a dark bulge, cocooned under her blanket, her knees pulled to her chest.

"Mami?"

Did one eye open?

"Mami?"

A hand rose weakly. It waved me away. I wanted to cry, but no tears came, so I slid back and lay sprawled across my mattress.

All around me I could hear the sounds of people retching. The baby in the next bunk wailed until I wanted to wail too, but I didn't because I remembered what the know-it-all woman had said about pigs on butchering day. I didn't want her to be right. In the darkness I heard someone's prayer: "Holy Mary, Mother of God, pray for us sinners. Holy Mary, Mother of God, pray for us sinners. Holy Mary, Mother of God..."

"Pray for us sinners," I finished when the voice stopped in mid-prayer.

That day bells clanged to call everybody to breakfast, and lunch, and dinner. If anyone went, I didn't see them go. The few people who weren't bothered by the ship's movements were sick from the stench of too many stomachs being emptied in the same space, at the same time. My only comfort came when I heard the know-it-all woman groaning and throwing up. There, I thought, she squeals just like everybody else.

On the second morning I was sitting cross-legged on my bed, holding the gnome's eye. The waves of

seasickness were fading, and as long as I sat still, my
stomach hardly hurt at all. Mami wasn't as lucky. She
was still curled up in her bunk.

"Make everything better. Make everything better.
Make everything better," I chanted softly, hoping
Martin's stone had some kind of power to help after all.

The white sheet that separated my bed from my
neighbor's shifted, and a small moon-faced boy with
a toothless grin peeked through.

"Are you talking to me?" he said.

"Why would I talk to you?" I snarled, feeling mean.

"What are you doing with that stone?"

I looked at his curious eyes and felt a little guilty.
"It's not a stone. It's a gnome's eye," I explained. "It has
special powers."

"It does not," he said, and I knew right then he had
no imagination.

"How would you know?" I snapped. "You're too
small to know anything. For your information, this
stone keeps away ghosts and monsters and all kinds
of scary things."

"You're silly."

"And you're stupid! Don't touch the curtain again
if you know what's good for you!"

I tucked the sheet back into place and pulled
my legs to my chest. With my chin on my knees,

I thought about how much I missed Martin and the Besselmeyers and our lager home.

Then I sighed. Sailing across the ocean was supposed to be an adventure. Now, as long as Mami was too sick to get out of bed, I was stuck in my bunk. Then I remembered that Martin wanted to know about the voyage. I decided to tell him.

Mami moaned softly as I climbed out of bed. "What are you doing?" she asked.

"Nothing. Just looking for something," I said, tugging my suitcase free from the net under her bed. She moaned again but didn't tell me to stop.

When I found a pencil and the postcards, I climbed back into bed and started to write.

Dear Martin:

We are on a ship called the Beaverbrae, *and I can tell you that it is not fun. You know how you said we would have a room of our own? There are no rooms, just rows and rows of beds.*

There is a six-year-old boy in the bunk beside mine. I call him Herman-the-Pest because he's all the time moving the white sheet between our beds and peeking at me. I don't like that he can see me when I'm sleeping and when I throw up. And what if he peeks when I'm getting dressed?

My stomach makes really loud gurgling sounds. You'd laugh if you could hear them. I'd laugh too, if the noises didn't come with cramps and the feeling that I might throw up again.

Beside me the curtain shifted. "What's that?" Herman asked as his head poked through the gap.

I pulled my sheet over the postcard. "Nothing," I said. What was the point in talking to a boy with no imagination?

Nine

On that second morning, some people got up when the breakfast bell rang. I wanted to get up too, but when I mentioned food, Mami groaned and turned her face into her pillow, so I stayed in my bunk until Tati came.

I saw him before he found us. He was weaving down the aisle, his arms reaching from one bed to the next to steady himself against the roll of the ship. He was checking the numbers stenciled on the beds, so I knew he was looking for us.

"Tati!" I called. I was happy to see him, but when he reached our bunk, I burst into tears. I don't know why, but my breath exploded from my chest, and I couldn't stop myself, even when I realized

Herman-the-Pest was watching and the know-it-all woman would hear.

My father hated tears. Sometimes when I cried he said, "Stop crying or I'll give you something to cry about." And then his hand would go up, just in case I didn't know what he might give me. But this time he handed me his handkerchief and said, "Here. Blow your nose. You'll see better." So I blew my nose and swallowed my tears, and then I got dressed while he talked to Mami.

"We need to get out of this stink hole," I heard him say. "Come, I'll help you so we can get out on deck and breathe."

She didn't want to go, but he coaxed her out of bed and helped her dress. I led the way up the steep staircase and out to the deck, where we turned our faces to the wind that bullied its way across the ship, and gulped in the fresh Atlantic air.

We watched steel gray waves roll toward us. They lifted the ship as they passed underneath, then rolled on until they met the steel gray sky.

Tati pointed out two lonely seagulls that wheeled above the ship.

"Will they cross the ocean with us?" I wondered.

He shrugged. The gulls floated down to roost in the rigging, but after a while they spread their wings and flew away. I wished I could fly. If I could,

I'd fly home. Back to the lager. Back to the Besselmeyers and Martin. Back to Oma. Even living with Oma would be better than sailing on this ship.

—◦◦◦—

Dear Martin:

For your information, there is no ballroom on this ship. There is a bar where the men sit and smoke and play cards, and there is a covered deck with long chairs so you can put up your feet. Sometimes Mami sits out there, but it's cold, and she has to cover up with the blankets from our bunks.

A sailor told Tati that our ship sails between Canada and Europe, but it only takes passengers when it's sailing to Canada. On the way back it carries cargo. I wonder what they do with our bunks then? Do they use them like shelves and fill them with boxes?

When you sail, take food. There's nothing here to eat.

That last part wasn't true. There was lots of food in the dining room. I just didn't like any of it. But once Mami felt better, she insisted that I eat every time the bells rang.

One meal was worse than the rest. It looked a little bit like goulash, but it had green and orange lumps and a thick brown sauce. The smell made my nose twitch.

"I don't want any," I said, even before the cook slapped some on my plate.

"Don't start," Mami warned.

I pinched my lips, and we carried our food to a long trestle table and sat down across from Herman-the-Pest and his family. They seemed to be enjoying their meal, so I tried some. It lay on my tongue, a damp, mushy mass, too awful to chew. Food juices seeped through my teeth and pooled at the bottom of my mouth.

"It tastes like boiled toad," I mumbled, keeping my tongue as still as possible so I wouldn't swallow by mistake.

"Don't talk with your mouth full," Mami scolded. Then she sighed and said, "*Du werscht noch Holzäpfel essa! Some day you'll have to eat wooden apples!*"

I didn't know what wooden apples might be, but I thought I'd like them better than the food on my plate.

There was nothing to do except spit or swallow, and I knew I couldn't spit, so I took a mouthful of milk to help everything slide down my throat. That's when Herman smiled one of his toothless smiles. A bubble of spit grew and popped in the corner of his mouth. The sight made me gag, and everything came back up.

My hand flew to cover my mouth, but milk sprayed from my nose and dribbled between my fingers, and little bits of food flew across the table. Some splattered right into Herman's plate.

"Go!" Mami said when I had stopped coughing and could breathe again. That day I left the dining room in disgrace. Later, when I thought it over, I didn't mind too much. After all, I didn't have to eat *my* dinner, and Herman had to stay and finish his.

⁓∰©

Every day Mami fussed because I didn't eat. I felt guilty about causing her worry. Not guilty enough to eat, just guilty enough to feel bad.

Sometimes Tati's sense of humor helped.

"Look at this," he said one day as he poked his fork at the meat on his plate. "The sign says we're having chicken, but this isn't chicken. What is it?" He bent and sniffed suspiciously. "It's dead, so I suppose we'll have to eat it. We don't want it to have died in vain." He put a small piece into his mouth and began to chew. "Definitely a bird of some kind. What kind of bird has tendons as tough as my razor strop?" He swallowed. "Aha!" he said. "Now I've got it! It's those silly seagulls. Remember the birds we saw in the rigging? That's what this is: seagull fricassee. Try it. You'll like it."

I laughed and ate a little, and when I went back to my bunk, I wrote another postcard to Martin, all about the seagull fricassee.

Ten

At first I was excited by the sign in the dining room:

> **FILM TONIGHT**
> 8:00 PM
> *Canada, From Sea to Shining Sea*
> FOR ADULTS ONLY!

"Adults only?" I complained when I read the last line. That's not fair. I'm going to Canada too!" I carried on until I saw the know-it-all woman giving me one of her fish-eyed looks.

Mami must have seen too. "That's enough!" she said in a low voice.

I pressed my lips together and didn't complain again...not until bedtime.

"You're going to leave me here?" I whispered, doing my best to sound pitiful. "Alone? Martin said this ship could sink in minutes if we hit an iceberg."

"That's really enough!" Mami said. Her voice stayed low, but her tone and her frown erased my last hopes. "Sometimes you have more imagination than brains!" she scolded. "Lie down and don't even think about getting out of bed!"

What could I do but obey?

One by one the grown-ups walked past my bunk until only the mother with her baby and the know-it-all woman were left in our aisle.

On the sheet beside me, Herman's shadow stretched and shifted until the lights were dimmed. I thought about going to sleep, but Herman-the-Pest started to make soft *Brrroom! Brrroom! Brrroom!* sounds. He went on and on. I could hear him even when I put my hands over my ears. It didn't help that he seemed to be having fun.

Finally, curious to see what he was doing, I hooked a finger around the edge of the curtain and pulled it aside just enough to peek at him. He was sitting up in bed, driving two pretend cars, one a cork and the other a bottle cap, up and down his knee-mountains. When the cork snagged on a fold of his sheet, it bounced and the bottle-cap car slid to the finish. Herman raised his arms in a silent cheer. That's when he saw me.

I hurried to tug the curtain back into place, but he poked his finger right into the middle of it.

"Stop it!" I warned. He pulled back, but then his whole head dove into the sheet, and he came into my bunk like a bedsheet monster.

A bubble of meanness rose in my chest, and I pulled my gnome's eye from under my pillow. Could I whack it on Herman's forehead? It would make a very satisfying *thwack*. That thought only lasted a second because I realized there would be tears and maybe even blood, and that would mean plenty of trouble for me, so I pushed the stone back into hiding.

Herman pulled back, but only long enough to attack again. This time the curtain stretched so far I was afraid it might rip from the rod and I'd have to sleep beside him without even a sheet for privacy. There had to be some way to stop him. I decided to try something Martin would do.

"Can't sleep?" I asked.

"What?" Herman paused, his head and shoulders halfway into my bed.

"I could tell you a bedtime story," I offered.

He pulled back.

"Of course it's a little scary, so maybe you don't want to hear it."

"I like scary stories," he said.

"It's a whisper story. You have to lie down and put your head close to the sheet to hear."

The blankets rustled, and then he whispered, "I'm ready."

I stretched out on my side of the sheet and began. "Way, way down in the deepest, darkest part of the *Beaverbrae* live creatures that only come out at night."

I kept my voice low, letting the story grow bit by bit. Telling it was fun, and he didn't seem to mind when I had to think about what to say next. Sentence after sentence the story got scarier and scarier, until it even made *me* shiver. For a while Herman stayed silent, but then his breathing seemed to get louder.

When I got to the part where the dark shadow leaned toward the sleeping child and began to suck on his ear, Herman started to whimper.

"You're not scared, are you?" I asked, pulling the edge of the curtain back.

Herman burst into tears. Who knew a small boy could make so much noise?

"Shhh!" I said, trying to calm him. "Shhh! It was only a story."

But Herman kept crying. I pulled the gnome's eye from under my pillow and held it out to him. "Here," I said. "Hold my stone. The magic will protect you."

He was reaching for it, and I'm almost sure that he would have stopped crying, but the know-it-all woman arrived. She must have stepped on the bottom bunk to look at Herman, because her face popped up right beside his. In the dim light her round green eyes seemed to wobble in her face. I thought I was looking at one of the night creatures from my story. "WAAAK!" I said, sounding like a chicken losing a tail feather.

Herman whirled. When he saw the know-it-all woman looming over him, his mouth opened as if he was taking a breath. But it didn't close. It stayed open until I thought, If he doesn't breathe soon he's going to fall over dead. When he did breathe, a howl came from his throat that would have shattered the windows if they hadn't had shutters.

That startled the know-it-all woman, and she fell back and crashed to the floor.

The baby began to wail. Children around us, who had been quiet, started calling out.

"What's wrong?"

"What happened?"

"Why is he crying?"

Some of them started calling for their mothers, and when nobody answered, they started to cry too. Things got pretty loud, and by the time the grown-ups came back from the dining room, the whole place was in an uproar. There was no point in pretending to be asleep.

I saw Herman throw himself into his mother's arms. "There, there," she kept saying. "What's wrong with my big boy?"

Every so often he pointed at me, and then at the know-it-all woman, but he was still crying, so nobody could understand what he was trying to say.

Then the know-it-all woman pointed at me and said, "That girl deserves a good spanking!"

Mami looked shocked. "Theresa? What happened? Did you hurt him?"

"No! I didn't touch him. Honest," I said.

"Well, then what?"

What could I say? "I didn't mean...I only wanted to..." None of those seemed like a good beginning.

"If she was mine, I'd give her a spanking to remember!" the know-it-all woman said.

"She's not yours!" Mami snapped back, and I was relieved until she went on. "I'll decide if she needs a spanking, and if she does, I'll take care of that too.

"Come," she said, helping me down from my bunk and leading me out of the sleeping quarters.

We went into the now-deserted dining room. From the look on Mami's face, I could tell she was angry. That wasn't good, because I knew how hard she spanked when she was mad.

"You'd better tell me what you did to make Herman cry."

"I told him to stop bothering me," I began. "He's all the time pulling the sheet back when I'm in bed."

"And that made him cry?"

"No…I think it was the bedtime story that made him cry."

"You told him a bedtime story?"

"Uh-huh. I wanted him to sleep so he'd stop bothering me."

"What story did you tell?"

"It's one I made up."

She groaned. "You made up a story? What was it about?"

"Oh, about some creatures that live in the hold of the ship."

"And?"

"And they come out at night when the moon is full to suck the wax from people's ears."

My mother's left eyebrow lifted, and she began to chew one corner of her lip. "I suppose one of the creatures sucked the wax from Herman's ear?"

"I didn't say 'Herman,' I just said 'a small boy with a round face.'"

Mami nodded. Her eyebrow stayed high and she chewed her bottom lip some more, but she didn't look nearly as angry as before.

"I'm sure he was going to stop crying, but then the…the tall woman came, and she climbed up to look at him and scared him even more."

My mother sighed. "You know that you have to apologize."

"I know. I'll tell Herman that the creatures…"

"No! Don't tell him anything. Promise me that you'll stop telling stories entirely."

So I promised. What else could I do?

Dear Martin:

I got in trouble yesterday. I thought about all the stories you made up, so I made up one of my own and told it to Herman-the-Pest, and now I have to stay beside my mother for a whole day. I thought it was a good story, but he thought it was scary. The funny part is that he cried again the next night because I wasn't allowed to tell him another one!

I'd write the story on a postcard, but it's way too long, so I'll write it on some letter paper and save it for you.

When Mami finally said I didn't have to stay beside her anymore, I got a sheet of paper and began to write.

Herman-the-Pest's Story:

Way, way down in the deepest, darkest part of the Beaverbrae *live creatures that only come out when the moon is full, like it is tonight. The moon calls to the creatures in the dark places, creatures that hide from the light of day.*

When the full moon rises, they rise too. Out from behind the trunks and boxes of the passengers, up from under the floorboards, through the metal railings and the sealed doors, they come: dark, floating shadows.

One by one they line up behind the last door, the door into the room where passengers are sleeping. Their hunger is huge. It chews at their bellies, bellies that have been empty since the last full moon.

Silently, they float into the room and through the aisles, down one row of bunks after another, until they find a sleeping child.

"This one is mine," one of the shadows whispers, and she stretches up until she is tall enough to reach into the high bunk. She leans toward the sleeping child, a boy child with a face as round as the moon in the sky.

The shadow bends down, and her fat lips cover the boy's tender ear. She begins to suck.

Plop! All the earwax pops into the creature's mouth.

"Mmmmm," she says softly. Then her long tongue slips in and out, and she licks all the tiny bits from deep inside the boy's ear.

I stopped writing because that was the point in the story when Herman began to cry. I wanted to think a bit more about what might happen next.

Eleven

For ten days there was nothing to see. Nothing but gray sky and dark water. On the eleventh day, there were birds floating in the sky like sleek, black kites.

"We're close," Tati said, and for a little while I was happy. This old ship knew the best way across after all, I thought.

The happy feeling didn't last, because little knots of worry started to form in my stomach as I thought about arriving in Canada. "What will happen when we get there?" I asked. I was asking my father, but some men standing by the railing overheard.

"Oh, there's sure to be a brass band!" one said. "Rows of people will come and line the dock to welcome us."

"*Ja, ja.* They'll bring flowers for everyone," said another.

"And they'll walk us down the main street of the city like in a carnival parade," added a third, and he did a little dance that made people nearby laugh.

I smiled at the thought, until I looked into their faces and realized they were joking. My shoulders drooped. I had so wanted to believe them.

Tati must have noticed, because he said, "Don't worry, Mouse. Whatever happens, we'll be fine."

When the men at the railing heard, they stopped laughing and turned away.

The next morning I knew we had arrived even before I opened my eyes. The engines were silent. The shutters were gone, and light streamed in from the salt-encrusted porthole by my bed. I lifted my head and leaned on my elbow for my first view of Canada. There it was: one long gray wall. I couldn't wait to find out what was on the other side.

—∞—

Dear Martin:

Today we boarded a train that will take us from Quebec City all the way to Toronto. The know-it-all woman will get off in Montreal. Imagine. She came all the way across the ocean to marry a man she doesn't even know. And he doesn't know her. Mami said she wonders which one will be most surprised. Herman-the-Pest and his family are going to Winnipeg. Tati said they will work on a sugar-beet farm to pay for their voyage, and then they'll be able to go where they want. Onkel Johann is supposed to meet us in the train station. I hope he doesn't forget.

Onkel Johann wasn't at the station when we arrived in Toronto. We stood together in the great hall, waiting, our eyes searching the crowd. My stomach tightened. What if…what if?

Then a voice called, "Adam! Aaa-dam!" and a man came striding through the crowd, his brown coat open, the sides flapping. He had a long green scarf wrapped loosely around his neck and a cloth cap that rested on his red curls.

"Johann," Tati called, and they walked toward each other, their arms wide. When they met, they laughed and hugged and slapped each other on the back. Then Tati turned away. I might have thought he was drying tears, but I knew he never cried.

Mami smiled and stretched her arms to hug and kiss Onkel Johann. "Thank you," she said, her voice so filled with relief that I realized she had worried too.

Onkel Johann had Tati's wide smile and high forehead, but he was a little taller and not so skinny. "Look at you!" he said, turning to me. "How you've grown." Then he hoisted me into the air as if I was a little girl. He laughed and turned round and round, right there in the station, until the whole world seemed to spin, and I felt happy and embarrassed at the same time.

"I see you've got your suitcases," he said when he put me down. "What about the rest of your things?"

"Our trunk is still in Quebec City," Tati explained. "It doesn't arrive until tomorrow. I'll have to come back for it."

"Good," Onkel Johann said, picking up Mami's suitcase in one hand, mine in the other. "Then we can go. It's a bit of a walk from here to my room, but it'll give you a chance to see something of the city."

He started out of the station at such a pace that Mami grabbed my hand and we had to hurry to keep up.

Outside I saw people climb into automobiles, others boarded red streetcars and some simply walked away. I heard their voices, but when I didn't understand their words, little worms of worry began to wriggle in my stomach. They didn't last long, because Onkel Johann looked so happy. Even if I don't understand, I thought, he does. I felt better.

Once we left the station, the people seemed to disappear, and Mami finally let go of my hand.

I was surprised at how deserted everything looked. The buildings were dark and the streets so empty that our footsteps echoed.

"It's so quiet," Mami said. "Where is everybody?"

"Nothing happens in Toronto on Sundays," Onkel Johann told us. "People go to church, and then they go home. Maybe in the summer we'll see some of them down there." He pointed, and when I looked to the bottom of a road that ran between a row of tall buildings, I was surprised to see water.

"We're still beside the ocean?" I said.

Onkel Johann laughed. "Not the ocean, Lake Ontario. It's big, but not as big as the ocean."

Just then the clouds parted, and sunshine dusted the gray waves, making them sparkle like gold.

"It's lovely," Mami said. "Lovely." And we all nodded our agreement.

Even with a suitcase in each hand, Onkel Johann walked fast. I was relieved when he led the way to a house with wooden stairs.

Inside there were more stairs that led to a landing, lined with doors. When Onkel Johann opened one of them I thought, Finally! We're here! But that door led to even more stairs, and we climbed until we reached a room at the very top of the house.

As soon as I stepped inside, I fell in love. It was a room for a princess; a tower room with windows that overlooked the street. The walls were painted a buttery yellow, and they curved in like welcoming arms. It was a bedroom and kitchen, all in one. In that room Onkel Johann had everything he needed: a bed, a stove, a chair, a table. There was even a wooden box attached to the outside of his window, where he kept a bottle of milk, some eggs and a package of sausages.

"My icebox," he said with a smile. "It keeps everything cold in the winter."

He pulled out the sausages and handed them to Mami. "I made these myself in the shop where I work," he said. "So many Europeans have been coming to our store that my boss is letting me add a little more pepper, some garlic and paprika. Even Canadians are buying them. I'm anxious to hear what you think."

"After the meals on the ship, we'll think they're delicious, won't we, Theresa?" Tati said.

Mami cooked the sausages with onions and sauerkraut on a tiny stove that Onkel Johann called a hot plate. Sauerkraut, I thought. Again. But this time the food tasted so much like home that I ate everything.

Later, I crawled into Onkel Johann's bed and fell asleep in minutes. Sometime during the night I woke to find Mami sleeping beside me. Tati and Onkel

Johann were on the floor, stretched out on a blanket, both of them covered with coats.

For breakfast Mami scrambled eggs, and we ate together before Onkel Johann went to work. We left at the same time, to find a home of our own.

Twelve

"**Y**ou won't have any trouble finding a place to live," Onkel Johann assured us. "Just look for signs like this." He printed the words *ROOMS TO LET* on a piece of paper.

He was right about the signs. They were tacked up in windows and on the posts of wooden porches.

Mami and I wanted to live in a nice house like Onkel Johann's, but when we found one, Tati shook his head. "Too much," he said. "We won't be able to afford the rent."

"Hmph," Mami said, putting her hands on her hips. "Then we'll have to keep looking."

We understood that people in all these houses had to share a bathroom, but in some places the kitchen had to be shared too. My mother didn't like that. "Sharing a bathroom is one thing," she said. "I'm used to that. But I'm not sharing a kitchen. Do you think I want strangers looking into my pots to see what I'm cooking? And look at this place! It's filthy!"

She waved her hand at three women clustered around a huge stove that stood in an alcove on the second-floor landing. The women stared back darkly. They began to mutter. Their angry looks made me reach for Tati's hand, but they didn't stop Mami's complaints.

"The whole house is full of foreigners!" she said. "For all we know, they might decide to poison our soup." Her voice dropped. "And besides," she said, "I won't be able to talk to a single one of them."

Tati tugged on her arm. "Come, Leni," he said. "We'll look somewhere else." I was relieved when he hustled us out.

Mami refused some places because the landlord or one of the roomers frightened her. "How could I sleep in this place?" she whispered as she led the way out of one house. "That man looks as if he would cut his own mother's throat."

That landlord glared as we walked away. He looked so mean that I couldn't help thinking she was right.

The next landlord frowned at me. "No children," he said, and when he saw we didn't understand, he shook his head. "No *kinder*," he said. We understood that, and I bit the inside of my cheeks and blinked away tears.

"It wouldn't hurt if you smiled, Theresa," Tati said.

"I'm too tired to smile," I grumbled.

"We're all tired," Mami said. Then she sighed. "Maybe it's just as well. A man who doesn't like children is not to be trusted."

The next house we found with a *ROOMS TO LET* sign was tall and narrow, and attached to another house just like it. Mami nodded, so we climbed the three steps to the tiny porch and knocked. A small, round woman answered. She was wearing a clean apron, and her white hair was pulled back in a tidy bun.

"*Komm herein. Komm*," she said, waving us in.

I was surprised when Tati hesitated. "We're...we're Danube Swabians," he said. "We speak German."

"Yes," she said, "I'm Jewish." And then she raised her eyebrows as if she was asking, Do you have a problem with that?

Mami stretched out her hand. "Leni Becker," she said. "And this is my husband, Adam, and our daughter, Theresa."

"Sniderman," the woman answered. "Hannah Sniderman."

Mrs. Sniderman and my mother hit it off right away, Mami talking in German and Mrs. Sniderman in something that sounded like German, but different.

"She's speaking Yiddish," Tati whispered when I tugged on his sleeve and asked why the words sounded strange.

Mrs. Sniderman led the way to a door that opened beside her own.

"Two rooms and a sunroom," she said, leading the way into a bedroom. "See?" she pointed. "Is big bed, and is couch. The girl, she can sleep there."

It was a large room, but not nearly as welcoming as Onkel Johann's. The walls were covered with paper patterned with vines and flowers, but their colors had faded, and the paper was all blotchy shades of brown. Next, Mrs. Sniderman led us into the kitchen. "Here is big stove *mit* oven. Is gas stove," she said, "and icebox." She pointed to the yellow box in the opposite corner. The icebox had two doors. A metal tray stood on the floor underneath. "This for ice," Mrs. Sniderman said, opening the top door. "This for food," she said, pointing to the other. "It works good."

There was a door in the wall beside the icebox. "What's in there?" I asked.

"Is sunroom," Mrs. Sniderman answered, opening the door so we could see.

The sunroom was a small space filled with odds and ends that looked old, used, and dusty in the light that streamed through the windows. It was so bright that, when we stepped back inside, the kitchen looked dark. I decided that a sunroom got its name because it trapped all the sunlight and kept it from shining into the rest of the house.

Mami walked to the sink and turned on the taps. She smiled when a stream of clear water came out, and her smile widened when she realized that the water flowed both cold and hot. "In Austria," she told Mrs. Sniderman, "I had to bring buckets of water from outside every day. Water for cooking, for cleaning, for laundry and for our baths. I'm happy if I never have to carry water again."

"Upstairs is bathroom too!" Mrs. Sniderman said quickly, now that she realized what would make my mother happy.

We went back to the hallway, and I led the way up the stairs, eager to see what this bathroom, right in the house, looked like.

"Look at the tub!" I exclaimed. "I can swim in there, it's so deep."

"It's long enough that I can stretch out and soak," smiled Tati.

Mrs. Sniderman didn't say anything until we stepped back into the hall. Then she gestured to the front of the house. "In this room," she said, "is three brothers from Ukraine. They working for railroad.

Is sometimes not home. This here is their kitchen." She pointed to the room at the back of the house. "Here," she said, pointing at the middle door, "is man too."

"There are eight of us in the house?" Tati said.

"Eight? Yes, eight if you move in," Mrs. Sniderman agreed.

"Eight people, one bathroom," Tati smiled wistfully. "That means there won't be time for soaking in the tub."

"Not time. Not water," Mrs. Sniderman said, sounding a little sad. "Everybody must sharing."

While my parents put their heads together and whispered, trying to decide if this should be our new home, Mrs. Sniderman placed her hand on my head. "Such hair," she said.

I cringed, thinking she was going to be like Oma and say how ugly red hair was. Instead she patted her own white bun. "When I am young, my hair is red too, but I have not such wonderful curls. My hair is red until my husband dies. He dies, and my hair turns white."

I peered at her. Hair as red as mine could turn white? That was a happy thought. I smiled at her, and she smiled back just as my parents agreed to move in.

Our first home in Canada: two rooms in a skinny, stuck-to-its-neighbor house on Kensington Avenue.

"It's not much," Tati said after we paid Mrs. Sniderman the twelve dollars for the first week's rent, "but better than the two rooms we had in the lager."

"We'll see," Mami said. "We'll see." But I thought she sounded pleased.

Thirteen

The next morning, Mami and I started to clean while Tati and Onkel Johann went to Union Station to pick up our trunk. I squeezed into the dark space under the kitchen sink and swept out dust and mouse droppings. While Mami scraped dirt from the walls of our oven, I washed the kitchen shelves. Together we washed windows and walls. We cleaned until our hands were red and wrinkled, and our rooms were filled with the smells of soap and vinegar. By the time Tati and Onkel Johann returned with our trunk, we were happy to stop cleaning and begin unpacking.

Mami's wooden noodle board, used for kneading and rolling out dough, came out first. At the sight of it, the day started to feel like Christmas. We took out the frying pan, the kitchen scale, two pots and the flour sieve. After that came our embroidered tablecloth and Oma's bedsheet, and from the folds of our duvet, we lifted Lissi and Oma's picture. Tati's sewing machine lay at the very bottom of the trunk.

"Thank goodness everything is dry and safe," Mami sighed as she stretched to hang Oma's picture on a nail over the big bed.

"Is it straight?" she asked, stepping back.

"It's straight," Tati said. "But I don't know...I'm not sure your mother looks happy there. Maybe we should put her in a more private spot."

Mami frowned, but she took the picture off the wall and tucked it back into the trunk.

I didn't object when Mami told me to put sheets on the couch right after supper. I was tired, and my parents must have been tired too, because they climbed into the big bed and went right to sleep. I lay still, listening to Mrs. Sniderman moving around her own small room beside ours. None of the noises she made sounded familiar, and I realized I was listening for Frau Besselmeyer's voice and Herr Besselmeyer's cough.

That night I dreamed I was in our barrack kitchen playing with a brood of fluffy chicks. The dream was so real I felt their tiny feet run across my fingers and their beaks peck, peck, peck seeds from my palm. When I heard a noise, I was sure it was Frau Besselmeyer knocking. "I'm coming," I said, sitting up. Then I realized where I was, and I was disappointed.

CLUMP! CLUMP! CLUMP! Someone was climbing the stairs. As I listened, the climber stumbled. A body hit the wall, making it shake. Angry words filled the night.

"Tati?" I whispered.

"It's nothing, Mouse," he whispered back. "Probably one of the men upstairs coming home."

"He's a very noisy man," I said.

"Drunk," Mami said.

"You don't know that," Tati objected.

"I know," she said. "I know."

When the footsteps reached the second floor, the hallway railing groaned. A door slammed. The toilet flushed. Pipes clanged. Doors opened and closed. And then, right over our heads, bedsprings squeaked as a body fell into bed. I held my breath. Silence. Then a heavy *THUD!* Maybe a shoe falling to the floor? When a second *THUD* came, Tati sighed, and I knew he had been waiting for the second shoe too.

For a long time I lay staring into the darkness. Then I turned. Turned again. Scratched one arm, then the other. Scratched my hand and my knee. I reached over my shoulder and scratched my back. Something skittered across my belly.

"Mami!" I gasped. "Mami! There's something in my bed."

The ceiling light came on, and when my mother whipped my blankets back, we saw a circus of small brown bugs dashing for darkness. I began to cry.

"Be quiet!" she warned. "You'll wake the whole house." Then she took my hand. "Come," she said more kindly as she led the way into the kitchen.

"We had bedbugs in the barracks after the war," she told me as she helped me slip off my nightgown. "I was hoping we'd never see another one. And now, here we are, halfway around the world and those little bloodsuckers are here before us!"

I stood naked and shivering while Mami wiped down my arms and legs. I was feeling sorry for myself until I saw her eyes fill with tears. "Don't cry," I said. "Don't cry. I'm all right. Really."

"Of course you're all right," she said, burying her face in the towel. When she lowered it, she smiled a tight smile and said, "We've dealt with bedbugs before, we can deal with them again."

"I haven't noticed any bites," she said to my father when we went back into the bedroom. "Do you have any?"

"A couple. I suppose your blood is sweeter than ours," he teased. "Or maybe this is bedbug party night in the old couch." He made room for me under the duvet. "Climb in," he said, so I did, and Mami slipped in after me.

"This is just like home," I said when we were settled again. I was remembering nights when frost spread feathery fingers across our windowpanes and the three of us piled up our blankets and the down-filled duvet and snuggled together to keep warm.

"It's better than home," Tati said firmly. "There's a furnace in this basement, and I saw a market up the street. After the war," he went on, "we had nothing; no meat, no milk, no fruits, no vegetables. We were lucky if we had bread."

Mami sighed. "It's true. You don't remember, but we used to line up at the soup kitchen. The only thing they had to feed us was soup made of beets and potatoes. The soup was thin and watery, and the beets were terrible. They had frozen in the ground before they were harvested, but we ate them anyway."

"I ate them too?"

"You did," Tati said. "When you're really hungry, you eat whatever you get."

"Even wooden apples?" I asked.

"Even wooden apples," Mami chuckled.

I smiled because I knew these stories. They were like family fairy tales, and most of them had a "happily ever after" ending.

"What else did we eat?" I asked, not wanting the stories to be over.

"One night we were so hungry we decided to go out and see if we could find something. Remember that?" Mami asked.

"How could I forget?" Tati said. "We were filling a sack with windfall apples and some onions from the farm on the other side of the river, when a dog started barking. The farmer came out and saw us scrabbling on the ground."

"You were stealing?"

"I'm afraid so. You were small enough that we were entitled to a liter of milk a week, but not extra food. We worried that you might get sick if you didn't get enough to eat."

"Was the farmer mad?"

"He lifted his lantern and looked at us, and when the light hit your face, you started to cry. He must have seen how scared you were."

"And how skinny," Mami added.

"Either way," Tati said, "he didn't say a word. Just turned around and took his dog into the house."

"He *could* have had us arrested," Mami finished.

"But he didn't," Tati said. "He was a good man."

"I don't like onions," I said.

"You didn't like them then either," Tati laughed.

"But when you're really hungry…"

"…you eat whatever you get," we finished together. Then we laughed, and for the first time since we left Austria, I almost felt as if we were home.

Fourteen

In the morning we told Mrs. Sniderman about the bedbugs. "*Oy vey,*" she said, shaking her head. "Bedbugs. Is not good." Then she raised one finger as if she had a thought. "You wait. We fix." She went into her room, rummaged about and came back with a brown bottle pump. "Is for killing bedbugs," she said, handing it to Tati.

"I see this is not the first bug in the house," he said as he looked at the pump.

"Is not first. Is not last too," she said with a shrug.

"The spray may work for the room, but not for the couch," Mami pointed out.

"The couch you carry to the street," Mrs. Sniderman said. "The garbage mens will take."

After some discussion it was settled that my parents would buy a new bed for me, and Mrs. Sniderman would take some money off the rent.

So the couch was hauled out to the curb, the mattress from the big bed was dragged into the yard and armfuls of bedding were hung on the laundry lines. When the room was bare, I was sent outside to sit on the narrow bench that ran along one side of the porch.

"Stay outside," Mami instructed. "And promise me you won't go anywhere."

I groaned, annoyed at her worry, but I promised.

For a while the street stayed empty, and I was soon bored and more than a little cold, so I made a game of jumping up and down the steps, first one, then two, then all three at once.

When a woman passed by, I smiled and called out, "*Grüss Gott*," like I always did at home. She didn't answer. But as she walked away, I realized that probably here in Canada people said different words for hello. I'd have to find out what they were.

Just then, a door opened in the house across the street, and a girl who didn't look much older than me came out. She looked my way. I looked back, hoping she would come to play, but she skipped down her steps and hurried up the street. She glanced over her shoulder once, but she didn't stop walking.

Inside our house a door slammed. I heard heavy steps coming down the stairs. That should have been a warning, but I didn't know that I was in the way until the front door whipped open and a man came storming out. He was in mid-stride when he saw me. I saw him raise his arms and do a funny little hop to keep from tripping over me, but by that time he was at the end of the porch, balancing on one foot like a tightrope walker. A sound like "AAAHRG!" came from his throat as he jumped to the pavement. It was only three steps down. I had been jumping them, no problem. But he landed badly and stumbled before he regained his balance.

He turned then, and shaking his finger at me, he spoke. I didn't understand his words, but I could see from his face that he was angry.

"*Verzeihung*," I said. "Sorry." My apology seemed to make him angrier. His voice got louder. I wanted to run, but I remembered Mami's warnings: *Stay outside*, and *Don't go anywhere*. I didn't know what to do. It was a relief to see Mrs. Sniderman raise her window. She said something to the man, but her words didn't help. His voice rose, and soon they were both shouting. Mami and Tati came to the door. When Mami's hands pulled me close, the man glared. His lip curled. He made a fist and waved it in the air. He said something that sounded like "Teepee!" Then he spat on the pavement and stalked away.

"I didn't—," I started, but I was interrupted by Mrs. Sniderman, who had come out of her room.

"This man..." She rolled her finger beside her head. "He crazy. He is finding new room. Is good he is going. He is noisy man."

It was a relief to know that I wasn't being blamed for what happened. Still, my heart was beating double-time because I knew the Noisy Man was mad, and I couldn't help feeling it was my fault.

"Tati?" I asked. "What did he mean when he said *Teepee*?"

My father shrugged, and we turned to Mrs. Sniderman for an explanation. "He is saying DP," she said in a low voice. "It means"—she paused—"it means Displaced Person. It means...people who have no home. He is angry. He is saying you will be taking away his job."

"He's a tailor?" my father said.

"Oh no. He is not tailor. He is nothing. He not keeping jobs because he is all the time drinking. He is not happy, and he blaming everybody for his trouble."

"There. Didn't I tell you he was drunk?" Mami said.

My question still wasn't answered. "Are we DPs?" I asked.

"Not this time," Tati said. "We were displaced after the war, when we came to Austria, but we applied to come here, and Canada accepted us as immigrants. We came here to work and live and to make a new home."

Not DPs, I thought. Still. Not Yugoslavian, not Austrian, not German and not Canadian either. It was hard to think we didn't belong anywhere.

We left the house then, to give the spray time to kill the bedbugs, but for the rest of the day I didn't complain when my mother kept me close to her side.

We walked all the way to Queen Street to buy my new bed. Mrs. Sniderman had told us the salesmen there spoke Yiddish and we would understand each other.

The furniture stores we saw were filled with amazing things, but the most amazing of all were the televisions. Martin had told me about televisions, but I had never seen one, and here, in Canada, the stores had rows of them for sale. I decided they worked with some kind of magic, like a movie in a box, and I wished Martin could see them for himself.

While I stared at the televisions, my parents talked to salesmen about beds and the barrel-shaped washing machines.

"What did he say?" Mami whispered as we left one store. "Did he say we can buy a washing machine with the money we have?"

"Yes, if we pay some now, and the rest at a dollar each week," Tati explained.

I thought the dollar-a-week plan was wonderful. We could use it to buy a television as well as a washing machine, but Mami was having none of it. "We're not buying what we can't pay for," she said. "Buy the bed. We need that. I'll wait for the washing machine." I couldn't imagine how many years it would be before we had enough money to buy a television.

We finally chose a bed that wasn't a bed at all. It was something called a davenport. The salesman showed us how it was a couch all day but it could be flipped open and flattened at night to make a bed. He showed us the space underneath where sheets and blankets could be stored when they weren't being used. And the best part was that it would be delivered the same day, for free.

We walked for a while before Mami said, "Did you see how the washing machine has a hose that attaches to the sink? Imagine not having to do laundry on the washboard ever again. Think how easy doing laundry will be with one of those. I wish I had one. I wish…"

"You'll get your washing machine as soon as I get a job," Tati promised. "Let's think of today as a bedbug holiday."

"Some holiday," Mami scoffed. "This day off just means extra work for me tomorrow, when I have to wash our laundry in the bathtub."

We walked until we came to a small store filled with groceries. "Do you think they sell soup?" she asked.

"Soup?" Tati said, leading the way. "Of course they sell soup. In Canada they have everything."

He was right. They did have everything. Inside, cans and packages lined the shelves. But nothing looked familiar, and we couldn't read the writing on the labels. Tati picked up a can. When he shook it beside my ear, it made a sloshing sound. "It sounds watery," he said with a wink. "It might be soup. What do you think?"

"For goodness sake, Adam," Mami scolded. "Who knows what's in there?"

Tati looked at the girl behind the counter and, in his very best German, asked, "*Fräulein, Haben Sie Hühnersuppe?*" He was asking the girl if she had chicken soup for sale, but she didn't understand. She smiled and looked puzzled, and then she said something that sounded like a question.

"*Suppe!*" Tati said a little louder. "*Suppe.*"

"Soup?" the girl said.

"*Ja! Hühnersuppe,*" he said, pronouncing every syllable.

The girl tilted her head as if she had trouble hearing.

To my surprise, Tati tucked his hands under his arms and began flapping them up and down as if they were wings. "*Kluck. Kluck. Kluck,*" he said, bobbing his head like a chicken pecking seeds. Then he stretched his neck, threw back his head and crowed like Frau Besselmeyer's rooster. "*Kikirikii! Kikirikii!*"

I groaned with embarrassment, but the girl laughed and went to a shelf. "Lipton Chicken Noodle Soup," she said, handing us a red and white box.

"*Lipton shicken noodle suppe,*" my father repeated. Then he said, "See, you *can* buy anything in this country. You just have to know how to ask."

On our way home we came to the market right at the end of our street. There were stalls filled with food, dishes, clothes, shoes and toys. One store sold only cheese, and another, only bananas. "I've heard that they're good to eat," Tati said.

"And they're pretty," I added. "Nine cents a pound. Is that a lot?"

"I don't think so," Tati said, and he bought one. He peeled away the golden skin, and right there in the store we had our first taste of banana. It was delicious.

Walking through the market was exciting, but I found myself looking around in case we met the Noisy Man. He was nowhere in sight. Neither was the girl from across the street, but I would have been happy to see her.

Fifteen

I wanted to go to school so badly that I didn't complain when Mami insisted that she be the one to comb and braid my hair. I didn't even complain when her comb snagged in my bed tangles. I was willing to suffer to go to school in Canada.

To get there, we walked along a busy street lined with stores that gave way to tall houses fenced from the street by stone walls. The school, which stood in the center of a cement yard, was a large red-brick building with wire-covered windows.

"Are you coming?" Mami said when I lagged behind. "I thought you couldn't wait to go."

"I'm…I'm scared," I whispered. My hand slipped into my pocket, where the gnome's eye lay.

Mami took my other hand. "It'll be all right," she said. "Everything new is a little frightening."

What could I do but follow? Inside, it was church-quiet and smelled of floor wax, dust, wet wool and things too foreign to recognize. Our footsteps echoed as we walked past a line of doors stained a dark chocolate brown. "Where are all the children?" I whispered.

"Probably in there." She motioned to the doors.

"So many?"

"I guess. The city must be full of children."

At the end of the hall, one door stood open. A nun seated behind a desk waved us forward. "Sister Mary Ursula," she said as she shook Mami's hand and accepted our immigration papers.

For what seemed a long time, she leafed through everything. She frowned, she sighed, she checked a book on her desk. Finally she folded her hands and peered at me from behind round, frameless glasses. I squirmed. A rumbling sound came from my stomach. I squirmed again. My hand reached for Mami's, but this time she brushed my fingers away and gave her head a small shake. I straightened. When the nun spoke, I was surprised that some of her words were German.

"The girl will be in grade three," she said. "*Dritte Klasse.* Until you learn English. When you learn, you can move up."

"Grade three?" I looked at my mother. That had to be a mistake.

"You're a smart girl, Theresa," Mami said. "You'll work hard. You'll learn. It will happen like magic. You'll speak English before your father and me."

The nun nodded.

I hardly heard. Grade three? Tears stung the back of my eyes. I wanted to say, "I'm almost eleven. I'm almost ready for grade six. You can't put me into a class with little kids," but my throat tightened, and I knew if I tried to speak, I'd burst into tears and humiliate myself.

We made a short procession on our way to the classroom: the nun, her hands tucked into opposite sleeves; Mami, her purse clutched to her chest; and me, one hand in my pocket, where my fingers curled around the gnome's eye. If it had any real magic, it would make this whole place disappear, I thought as Sister Mary Ursula knocked on one of the dark doors.

It opened, and I stared. Did Martin's stone have some magic after all? A woman was smiling down at me. She had red hair. Not red and curly like mine. A beautiful shade of red that shone like gold. It fell to her shoulders in graceful waves. Nice, I thought.

She looks nice. Right then I decided to give this school a chance. Maybe it would be all right. And when Mami handed me the paper bag that held my lunch, I took it and didn't complain.

I wasn't the biggest student in the class. At the back of the room there was a boy who was so tall his legs stretched into the aisles from both sides of his desk. His black hair stuck up in dry, untidy clumps, and I knew if Mami saw it, she would shake her head and say, "That head needs to meet a comb."

The teacher led me to the desk beside his, and I sat. I kept my eyes on her face and did my best to understand the words that came from her mouth. She spoke slowly, her lips stretching out the sounds. I watched and listened, but I didn't understand. I didn't understand.

You'll learn to speak English. It will happen like magic, Mami had said. *Like magic.*

I waited, but no magic happened.

The teacher gave me a pencil, a box of crayons and a page filled with empty squares. I wondered what to do with them. When I glanced at the boy beside me, he scowled.

The girl in front of me was filling her boxes with drawings, so I leaned forward and copied her.

By the time I finished the first box, the girl was curving her arm around her paper. I had to stretch to see the rest. She didn't like that. I could tell, because she turned and gave me an angry-owl glare, and then she stuck out her tongue. I might have stuck out my tongue at her, but she looked so silly that I only stared. She didn't like that either, and her small mouth made a tight little O. Then her hand went up, and she whipped it back and forth.

"Dorothy?" the teacher said.

I didn't need to understand English to know that the words pouring from Dorothy's mouth were about me.

A knot formed in my stomach, and I waited to see how I would be punished. As it turned out, the teacher's words were all quiet ones, and when she was done, Dorothy moved her arm and let me copy the rest. When a bell rang, everybody lined up; me and the really big boy were at the end.

The teacher waved me forward to stand beside Dorothy. She said something, and Dorothy took my hand as if she was going to be my friend. She held my hand all the way down the hall, but as soon as we walked outside, she let go and made a big show of wiping her hands on her coat, as if holding mine had made hers dirty. Then she laughed and ran away.

In the schoolyard I stood pasted against a wall watching girls untangle ropes. Some had small rubber balls to play with. All of them seemed to be laughing. The more they laughed, the worse I felt.

When I saw the girl from the house across the street, I straightened, hoping she'd come and talk to me. She saw me. I know she did, but just then another girl tapped her shoulder, and she turned and raced away. They were playing tag. I wished I could play. I pretended I was happy to stand alone.

Then my eyes found the gate in the schoolyard fence, and I stopped pretending and began to run. I ran from the shouts and the happy voices. I ran until I reached the corner. Then I stopped running, but I kept walking.

I would go home and tell Mami that I couldn't go back. "I don't belong there," I would explain. "No one likes me there. I am never going back." Mami would understand. She wouldn't make me go back. Not ever.

Every once in a while I saw something I had noticed on our way to the school: the house with a big tree in front, a brick wall that fenced another, a porch with a swing.

When I arrived at a big street, I remembered the lights, the streetcar tracks, the overhead wires. I remembered the shoe store and the restaurant on the corner. Cars streamed by. Bells clanged. A streetcar rumbled through the intersection. The lights turned from green to red.

"Cross with the green light," Mami had said. "Cross with the green light and walk carefully."

A blue car turned the corner. Startled, I jumped back. When it was gone, I pulled the gnome's eye from my pocket. I was not going to be a mouse. I would cross this street and get home safely.

The green light flashed on, and I stepped off the sidewalk. It was a wide street. Two lanes for cars to go one way, two lanes with tracks for streetcars, two more lanes for cars going the other way. I kept walking. A man started to cross from the other side. He came shambling toward me, a shopping bag hanging from his hand. His shoulders were hunched and his head hung low, but there was something…something about him I recognized. He looked up, and then I knew. It was the Noisy Man.

I paused, but only for a second, before I whirled and hurried back to the sidewalk. I ran all the way back to the schoolyard. It was empty except for a few students and a teacher beside the door. When she saw me, the teacher shouted and waved. I ran and slipped inside. I didn't want to be at school, but right now I didn't want to be outside either.

~ ❦ ~

At noon I saw the girl from across the street again, and this time she smiled and waved me over. "Lydia," she said, tapping her chest. "Lydia," she said again.

"Lydia," I echoed.

She pointed at me. "Theresa," I said.

"Hey, everybody. This is Theresa. She lives on my street," she said to her friends as she thrust the handle of a rope at me. She wrapped her fingers around mine. "Turn, turn, turn," she said, moving my arm until I had the rhythm. The other girls smiled and laughed and sang as they jumped. I was happy to turn. It was better than standing alone.

"I had a great day," I told my parents that evening. "Some girls showed me how to jump with a rope, and I learned lots of English words. Can I have a rope too? Everybody has a jumping rope."

"Take a breath, Theresa," Mami said. "Give your father a chance to wash his hands. You can tell us the rest later."

As it turned out, my news had to wait because Mami was more interested in hearing about Tati's new job.

"It's in a factory," he explained. "They make jackets for men. Someone does all the cutting. I'll just sew. They pay by the piece. The faster I work, the more I can earn."

"Is that good?" Mami wanted to know.

Tati's eyebrows came together and worry lines creased his forehead. "I'm used to making suits to measure. I'll have to get used to working fast."

He turned to me. "Tell us your news," he said.

"Do you know," I started, "English is a funny language. They say *Haus* and *komm* almost like we do. And I learned some new words: *pencil* and *turn* and *jump* and *recess*. And I learned a brand-new word from the girl who sits in front of me. Do you want to hear it? *Shut up!*"

Everybody smiled, and I was happy. I was learning English. It was not happening like magic, but still…

I went on to tell about other things that happened that day, but I left out the part about running away at recess. What was the point? It would only make Mami worry.

Sixteen

We were standing at the kitchen table, Mami slicing onions while I peeled potatoes for our dinner. "Watch your peels," she warned as she lifted her cutting board to carry the onions to the stove. "If you don't make them thinner, there won't be enough potato left to cook."

I peeled more carefully, but when the potatoes were done, I started talking, my voice loud enough to be heard over the sizzle of onions in the pan. "My desk is the very last one in the row. It's right beside a boy's. His name is Roberto."

"What kind of name is Roberto?"

"Italian, I think. Mostly he talks to the other Italian kids. He hardly talks to anybody else. All he does is slouch in his chair, and when the teacher's not watching, he carves his name into his desk.

"The funny thing is, I think our teacher likes him. I don't know why, because, you know, he's really disgusting. His nose runs all the time, and he's always wiping it on his sleeve."

"Try not to look."

"Ha! Do you know how hard that is? He snorts, and then he makes this really disgusting *snurgking* sound. Really. He does it loud and all the time. You can set your clock to it. I know, because I started counting. One, two, three, four, five, *SNURGK*! One, two, three, four, five, *SNURGK*! One, two, three…"

"Enough!" Mami warned. "I don't want to hear any more."

I sighed. The story about Roberto would have made Martin laugh. He would have made *snurg-king* sounds of his own and maybe made up a story about a boy who turned into a pig. But here in Canada there was nobody who wanted to hear my stories, and nobody to tell me theirs. For a while I sulked, annoyed that Mami wouldn't listen.

The kitchen filled with the burbling sound of water boiling and the splatter and crackle of the onions frying. My nose wrinkled at the smells, and when Mami added liver to the pan I groaned. Onions were bad enough. Liver and onions…only sauerkraut was worse than that.

Still, I didn't want to lose my talking time, so I tried again. "Our teacher brings a chair and sits down between our desks when she helps us with our work. Sometimes she even takes Roberto's hand and helps him write letters or numbers. Do you think she doesn't know how often that hand has crossed his nose?"

I glanced up. Mami was busy at the stove.

"Sometimes his *SNURGK!* is really long and loud, and then he wipes his sleeve across his face because the stuff from his nose has dripped too far down to be sniffed up."

"Theresa! That's disgusting."

I knew I should stop, but I added, "Maybe he's never heard of handkerchiefs."

"Maybe he doesn't have one," Mami said. "I'll give you one of your father's. You can give it to him. It might help."

"I can't give Roberto a handkerchief! I hardly know him. What if he gets mad?"

"Then I suppose you'll have to suffer in silence!" she said.

As it turned out, it was the teacher who gave Roberto a handkerchief, a brand-new blue handkerchief with a darker blue border. She slipped it across his desk and whispered something I couldn't hear. I don't think anybody else even saw.

"Thank goodness!" I told Mami that evening. "Now he won't have snail tracks up and down his sleeve."

"You could follow your teacher's example and be kinder to Roberto," she said. "You might make a friend."

"But he's a boy!"

"So was Martin."

"Roberto is nothing like Martin. How can you even think we might be friends?"

"What *I* think is that you need to understand that every friend you make will be different. If you expect them all to be like Martin, you won't ever have a new one."

I opened my mouth to argue, but no words came out. What could I say anyway?

—◌◌—

At school there was so much to learn, so much I didn't understand. Most of the time I watched and listened, but I was afraid to say anything. Afraid I might say even words I knew the wrong way. People would laugh. I made up for not talking at school by talking nonstop at home.

"You remember that boy, Roberto?" I said at supper one evening. "He must be really stupid. He's been in Canada longer than me and he can hardly do anything!"

Tati frowned. "Maybe not stupid," he said. "Maybe he's never been to school before."

"But that can't be. He said he's almost twelve!"

"If he grew up in a village, there might not have been a school. During the war, schools were bombed like a lot of other buildings. Sometimes it took years before they were rebuilt. Some children didn't get a chance to learn. Not everyone was as lucky as you."

Tati's words made me feel like a bag with all the air sucked out, and I wished I could take back my own.

I started to watch Roberto. It didn't take long to see what he couldn't do, so I began to help him. We started with numbers. We didn't need a lot of English words for that. Our teacher noticed. She smiled, so we went on, even when Dorothy stuck out one pointing finger and rubbed the other one over it. I didn't need to speak English to understand the finger of shame, but since I didn't like Dorothy anyway, I ignored it.

Roberto started teaching me a few English words. I was surprised at how many he knew, because I had never heard him talk in class. I guess he was just as embarrassed as I was to talk in front of the other kids.

It was Roberto who told me that our teacher's name was Miss Lamb. And he told me *lamb* meant baby sheep.

—⁂—

"Miss Lamb is just like her name," I told my parents that evening. "Really. She's so nice. Do you know she never yells? Not ever. Not even when somebody spilled paint and Dorothy walked through the puddle and made orange footprints on the floor."

Sometimes, when Miss Lamb was busy, Roberto and I took two chairs and some books into the cloakroom. We looked at pictures, pointing and saying words: *tree, cat, dog, house, street, butterfly, bird*; everything we had words for. Sometimes we just talked, and even though some of Roberto's words came out in Italian and mine in German, we understood each other.

One day Roberto said, "My papa, he work in restaurante. I work too. I peel da potatoes. I wash da dishes."

"You get paid money?"

"My papa get da money. I get da food."

At home I tried to sound very grown-up as I shared this news. "Do you know that Roberto works in a restaurant after school? He even gets paid, but his father keeps the money. I don't think that's fair at all."

"Fair?" Tati said. "What makes you the judge of what is fair? The boy's family is probably trying to save for their future. For Roberto's future. I'm sure his father needs every penny of the boy's earnings."

I thought about how little money we had.

"Should I get a job?" I asked.

"Job!" Mami cut in. "You have a job. Your job is to go to school and learn something. That's your job! See that you do it well!"

My chin dropped. Some days I couldn't say anything right.

⸺❦⸺

One Saturday Tati came home with a pad of paper. "Here, Mouse," he said, "it's for you. It was on sale," he explained when Mami complained about the extravagance.

I fanned the pages. They were fresh, white and so clean they asked to be written on. "Is there something you want me to write?" I asked, pleased with the gift.

"Start with a letter to the Besselmeyers," Mami said. "I promised to send mail, but it's all I can do to write to your oma each week. I'm just too tired. If you're writing anyway, you might as well write something useful."

So I wrote:

Hello Herr Besselmeyer und Frau Besselmeyer,

This is Theresa writing to you all the way from Toronto, Canada.

Toronto is nothing like home. It is full of houses and people and cars, and there is even a big market on our street called the Jewish Market. Mrs. Sniderman, our landlady, says it's because the people here used to be mostly Jewish, but now there are lots of other people too. Like us.

There is even a synagogue. Do you know what that is? It is a place for Jewish people to pray. The men who go there wear long black coats and round black hats, and they have curls beside their ears.

Mrs. Sniderman does not go there. Every Friday she goes to visit her daughter, and they pray in a different synagogue.

Our church is called St. Patrick's, and the priests there speak German, so we understand everything. They are very nice, but Father Kelly is the nicest. He comes to our school and tells jokes. I think he likes me. He said my hair is like a halo.

This week we bought a washing machine. I catch the clothes when they come through the wringer so that they don't fall back into the water.

How are your chicks? They must have all their feathers by now. We buy our chickens in the market. You can point to the one you want, and the man in the store will take it out of the crate and kill it, and pluck it, and clean it for you. And then you can take it home naked, with the head gone, but the feet still attached. Mami says that is much easier than doing all the work yourself. But she says that the chickens here don't taste the same as the ones at home.

You can read this letter to Martin. Tell him our address so he can write. I will write another letter and send him his postcards as soon as I have the money for the stamps.

Love, Theresa

Mami made me recopy the whole thing. I had to write small to get all the words on one page, and we mailed it right away.

Seventeen

There wasn't much my mother didn't notice. One afternoon she was standing at the sink peeling apples, the peels falling from her knife in long, thin spirals, while I stood, one leg crossed in front of the other, bouncing.

"What are you doing?" she asked.

I squirmed.

"Do you have to pee? For goodness sake! Go! What on earth are you waiting for?"

"I'm scared," I whispered.

"Scared? What do you mean, scared? I'll give you something to be scared of if you wet your pants!" She grabbed my hand and hurried me to the door. "Run!"

I stumbled up the stairs, into the bathroom and across to the toilet, lifting my skirt and dropping my underpants as I went. I was sitting when Mami came to stand in the doorway. "Flush," she said when I was done. "Now, tell me what this is all about."

I blinked away tears. I didn't want to make things worse by crying, but a sob escaped my throat, and I had to take a breath before I could say, "It's dark up here. And quiet. The doors are always closed. And there's no window, and now the light doesn't work." My throat made a gulping sound. "And I'm all the time worried about…" I pointed to the door of the Noisy Man's room.

Mami shook her head. "The man moved out days ago! Honestly! There are times when I worry that you really do have more imagination than brains! You're scaring yourself silly, just like you scared Herman."

I looked at the empty hallway. Did I have more imagination than brains? With my mother beside me, I could see there was nothing up here that was scary. Why was I always so afraid?

"We'll ask Mrs. Sniderman to put in a new bulb," Mami said, taking my hand as we started back down. "And we won't have any more of this nonsense, will we?"

Mrs. Sniderman put in a new bulb, but it must have been a small one, because the hallway didn't look much brighter, and I was still afraid to go upstairs alone. That's why I started carrying the gnome's eye for every bathroom trip.

It will protect you from all things evil, living or dead, Martin had said. I knew it wouldn't. There was no magic in stones. Still, its weight and its cool, hard surface in my palm gave me a little courage, and I decided that if something jumped out at me from behind one of the doors, I could use the stone to protect myself.

The next morning I was on my way upstairs when I heard grunting noises coming from the bathroom. I stopped, straining my ears to listen until I heard, *"Oy vey!"* Was it Mrs. Sniderman? Pasting myself to the wall, I edged up, one step at a time, my neck stretching until I could see.

It was Mrs. Sniderman. She was folded over the side of the bathtub like a paper clip, her head and arms in the tub, her toes straining to stay in touch with the floor. From where I stood, I could see the tops of her brown stockings rolled into little sausages just below her knees, and the material of her dress tight over her hips. She was cleaning the bathtub.

"*Immer Arbeit.* Always work," I heard her grumble.

I slipped the gnome's eye into my pocket before she straightened and looked my way. I suppose she knew what I wanted, because she said, "Come. You pee. I finished."

She lifted her bucket of cleaning supplies and moved into the Noisy Man's room while I scurried into the bathroom.

When I was done, I heard Mrs. Sniderman still grumbling. "*A Chazer shtal!* A pigpen!"

Curious, I tiptoed along the hall and peeked around the doorframe of the Noisy Man's room. It was small, dark and narrow, the walls faded to a shade of grayish green, not unlike the color of our kitchen. A skinny window faced the neighbor's red-brick wall. The window was closed, and the air in the room was thick with a musty, dead-mouse smell. As I watched, Mrs. Sniderman lifted the sash and wedged a piece of wood underneath to prop it open.

"Come," she said, when she saw me. "Come. He is move out."

I watched her shake open a brown paper bag, then shove her mop under the bed. When it reappeared, it was dragging dust balls and a collection of litter. I grimaced as I bent to help. With my thumb and first finger I picked up an old sock, a dirty undershirt, the scrunched wrapper from a Sweet Marie bar, an apple core—shriveled, brown and hard—and two empty Players cigarette boxes. One by one I dropped everything into Mrs. Sniderman's paper bag. She mopped the rest into a pile and pushed it into her dustpan before she turned to pull the blanket from the bed.

"Ech! Look at this," she said, poking her finger through a brown-edged hole in the blanket. "*A chazer bleibt a chazer*. A pig stays always a pig. You not smoke in the bed, I tell him. You not smoke in bed, or we all burn! He is not listening. Is good he is move out. You look what is there." She pointed to the low, battered dresser beside the bed.

I slipped behind her and pulled on the first drawer. It was stiff, and it squealed as it came out in uneven jerks. There was nothing inside except a sheet of yellowed newspaper that lined the bottom, so I closed it again and pulled on the second drawer. That one came flying out and crashed to the floor.

Mrs. Sniderman turned, her lips a hard line. At first I thought she was annoyed with me, but it turned out to be the rows of small brown bottles in the drawer that were making her frown.

"Is good. Nothing is broken," she said, and she sent me to carry bottles out to the garbage can beside the house. I carried them, two at a time, and made seven trips up and down the stairs. When we lifted the drawer and pushed it back into place, the newspaper liner shifted and a photograph slipped out. It was a picture of a man standing beside a woman and two small boys. Behind them was a garden with a fence and a tree.

"Is that the Noisy Man's family?" I asked.

"Yes. Before."

"Before?"

"Before he walks the wrong road."

"Will he go back to them?"

"No. He don't go there. When people walk the wrong road, they not going back. This man, he follows the little brown bottles, not his heart, not his head."

I wasn't sure I understood what she meant, but I understood the sadness in her voice.

She turned to bundle the bedsheets while I knelt on the floor and looked under the dresser. I found two things buried in gray fuzz: a bent teaspoon and a small coin, a dime. When I held them out to Mrs. Sniderman, she took the teaspoon, but she rolled my fingers over the dime.

"You keep. You save for special," she said as she heaped the bundled sheets into my arms and directed me to carry them downstairs too. I smiled all the way down. My arms were full of smelly sheets, but the dime in my hand was filling my mind with possibilities. A whole dime!

"I hope you're not going to let it burn a hole in your pocket," Mami said when I showed her the money.

I shook my head. "No. I'm going to save it for special, like Mrs. Sniderman said."

The coin went into the small box I kept hidden inside the davenport. I had been planning to keep all my treasures there, and now I had two: the gnome's eye and a dime. But the money didn't stay in the box for long. On the first really hot day, I spent it at the bakery up the street for an extra large, double-dip, strawberry ice-cream cone. I decided that was special enough.

Eighteen

A new tenant moved into the Noisy Man's room. His footsteps slippered across the floor above us: *schlup-schlup, schlup-schlup, schlup-schlup*; back and forth, back and forth; one, two, three steps one way; three, two, one steps back.

"Doesn't that man ever sleep?" Tati grumbled.

The noise of the new tenant's footsteps didn't bother me. I liked the rhythm. It lulled me to sleep.

One afternoon, when I was passing Mami clothespins to hang our laundry on the lines, Mrs. Sniderman joined us in the yard. She began talking about the new tenant.

"He is relative," she explained, "from my sister. He is the uncle of the brother-in-law, from her husband."

My forehead wrinkled as I tried to figure out the connection. It was too hard for me.

"He is alone now," she went on. "His wife, she is died. They haf a daughter, Sarah. She vas lost in Russia." Mrs. Sniderman sighed. "Is long time ago, now. Sarah vas small. Like Theresa. Was very bad time." She sighed again.

Mami was holding a towel to the line as she took the clothespin I held out. I watched her expression change from curiosity to sadness. "It's a terrible thing to lose a child," she said.

Then, turning to me, she said, "Go. Go and play before it gets too dark," and she shooed me out of the yard. I went, but I didn't think it was fair to be sent away just when they were going to talk about something I wanted to hear.

~❦~

Almost a week passed before I saw the new tenant.

I was making one of my last-minute dashes for the toilet, holding the gnome's eye and whispering, "I'm not scared. I'm not scared." In my hurry I didn't look where I was going, and I crashed headfirst right into a man's soft middle.

He grunted. Water sloshed from the pot he was holding. The gnome's eye flew from my hand.

I scrambled for it right through the puddle. When I stood up, my hands and knees were wet, and I found myself face-to-face with a little man. For a second or two, his dark eyes stared right into mine. I thought he smiled as he stepped aside to let me pass. I slipped around him and ran into the bathroom, slamming the door as I went. I didn't have time to be polite.

When I was done, I flushed, and this time, instead of racing down, I tiptoed into the hallway. It was empty. The floor was dry, and all the doors were closed. Then I thought I heard a voice. Was it whispering my name? Was it? I grabbed the newel post, whipped around and flew down the stairs.

One day I was halfway through my regular dash down the stairs when I heard a light *plink, plink, plink*, as something tumbled down beside me. I heard it, but I was already in our bedroom, my heart racing, before I stopped to think what it might be.

After a while I opened our door and peeked out. There was a caramel on the third step. One of those light brown, cellophane-wrapped candies that start off hard but glue themselves to your teeth and the top of your mouth when they get soft. I recognized it. It was the same kind of candy Frau Besselmeyer used to buy for me at our lager store. I went out, picked it up and stretched my neck to see who might have tossed it down. Upstairs, everything looked dark.

"What have you got there?" Mami asked when I came into the kitchen. I showed her the candy and explained that it came from the little man who lived upstairs.

"Put it back!" she said, the anger in her voice surprising me. "Don't ever take candies from strangers. Never, never, never. You *never* know…," she finished, leaving me to wonder what I didn't know.

She followed me into the hallway as I climbed up and left the caramel on the post.

The second time I saw the Little Man, it was his reflection I recognized. I was waiting beside the bakery window while Mami bought bread inside. I had been trying to decide which cake I would choose if we had money to buy a cake, when I saw him. He was on the opposite sidewalk, holding a cloth bag. Lydia came by just then, and I was so pleased to see her that I pointed at the little man's reflection. "New tenant," I told her. "He walk every night." I demonstrated, counting "One, two, three," as I marched one way. Then, "One, two three," as I marched back.

She laughed. "That one?" she asked, pointing. "The one that looks like a buzzard?"

"Buzzard? What is buzzard?"

"It's a big black bird that stands all hunched over. It has a long neck that folds down so the head is way down here between its shoulders."

She lifted her shoulders and pulled her head down and forward to show me what a buzzard looked like. Then she let her top lip drop over the bottom and scrunched her eyes together. She looked so funny I began to laugh.

Lydia giggled too. "Look at him," she said. "Buzzard is a good name for him."

It's true, I thought, looking across at the Little Man. His neck droops, his shoulders droop, even his eyelids droop. "Buzzard," I said out loud, and then again. "Buzzard." The word tickled.

All this time the Little Man was leaning against a post as if he was catching his breath. When he saw me looking, he smiled and raised a hand in greeting. I turned back to the store window, pretending I didn't see. Why did the new tenant have to be so funny-looking?

And then, through some trick of the light, the cakes behind the window disappeared, and I found myself staring at my own reflection. My hair, neatly braided in the morning, had long since worked itself loose and was framing my face in a cottony cloud of red. My glasses had slipped to the end of my nose, and there was a smudge on my forehead. I sighed, wet a finger to wipe away the smudge and pushed my glasses back into place. The Little Man was not the only funny-looking tenant in our house.

More caramels appeared on the newel post after that. I decided they had to come from the Little Man, because sometimes when I found them, I knew he was the only other person home. The caramels were never there when I went up, but sometimes one was waiting for me when I was ready to go back down.

I ate the caramels. Eating them made me feel guilty because I was disobeying my mother, and even worse, because I was accepting a gift from someone I had called "Buzzard." But they were so sweet. It was hard to pass them up.

Nineteen

very morning Tati left early and walked to work.
"I sit all day," he told us. "I need the exercise."
But I knew the real reason he walked was to save the
streetcar fare.

He told us that he spent his days sewing jackets:
twenty-four a day; more if he was lucky enough to get
overtime. Overtime meant he could stay longer and
sew more jackets to make more money.

Most Saturdays he worked at a different job in a
small tailoring shop, where he sewed suits. He liked
that job. "There is a satisfaction when you make something from scratch that you don't get when you sit
and sew seams," he told us. But even when he worked
six days a week, he never made enough. I could tell,

because Fridays almost always ended with arguments, and all the arguments were about money we didn't have.

On Fridays Tati stopped at the bank to cash his paycheck. When he came home, he put the money on the shelf over the sink until I was in bed. That's when my parents began to whisper. They whispered as they counted the money. They whispered as they put aside what they needed for rent and groceries, for shoes and clothes, and for everything else. Then they whispered about how much was left over to save. Those whispers were never happy ones. They slid out of the kitchen with short, sharp, hissing sounds that sliced like knives. Sometimes the whispers were followed by a stone-heavy silence. One Friday they were followed by the sound of dishes shattering.

I bolted up.

There was a second crash. "*Herr Yemini!*" Mami shouted, and I knew she was mad. "This is how you save?" she went on. "By breaking dishes? If it's broken dishes you want, I'll help you break them!"

There was a third crash, and I bounded out of bed and ran to the kitchen. I got there in time to see my mother raise both hands and hurl another plate to the floor, sending shards skittering across the room.

"Mami?" I said.

My parents turned to me, their eyes wide.

It was Mami who spoke first. "Don't move," she said. "You'll step on something." And I watched her walk to the sunroom as Tati came and scooped me up to carry me to bed.

"Lie down, Mouse," he said as he brushed his hand over the bottom of my feet. "You need to go to sleep."

"Are you going to break more dishes?"

"Not today," he whispered. "Your mother and I will make peace." But I saw him comb his fingers through his hair, and I knew he was still angry.

When I lay down, he pulled my blanket up and stretched his lips into what was supposed to be a smile. I tried to smile back, but he turned away.

From the kitchen came the scratchy sounds of china being swept off the floor. Tati didn't go to help. He opened the bedroom door and walked into the hallway. At first I thought he was going upstairs, but when I heard the front door open and close, I knew he was leaving.

In the kitchen I heard my mother blow her nose. I knew what that meant. It was a long time before the lights were turned off and she climbed into bed.

"Mami?"

"Go to sleep."

"Is he coming back?"

"Of course he's coming back. He has no place else to go."

"What if he takes the wrong road?" I asked, thinking of the Noisy Man.

She didn't understand. I could tell, because she said, "Your father knows his way. He won't take the wrong road."

I tried, but sleep didn't come until Tati's key turned in the lock and his shadow crossed the room. I watched him climb into bed and heard him whisper. Then I turned over and went to sleep, because the new whispers were so soft they didn't hurt at all.

Not long after that, Mami announced, "A woman at church told me about a job. I'm going to take it. We can't live on Kensington Avenue and count pennies forever. The only way we'll get ahead is if I go to work too."

She took that job, and it wasn't long before she had another, and another. Soon she had a job for every day of the week. She told us that she took the streetcar, the subway and a bus to travel to the streets where rich people lived, and where she spent her days cleaning their houses. Five houses, five days a week, a different house every day.

Lucky for us, there are lots of rich people in Toronto who can pay her five dollars a day to clean up after them, I thought.

But I never felt lucky when she left in the morning, because as soon as the door closed behind her, the house began to whisper. It sighed and creaked and groaned. I was afraid of the noises, so as soon as she was gone, I left for school. More imagination than brains, I thought, every time I locked the door behind me. But no matter how I tried to tell myself that there was nothing in the house to hurt me, all it took was one creak to suck away every ounce of my courage.

At school I learned to say, "Can I play?" When I did, girls almost always nodded and let me join in their games. Everybody except Dorothy.

Once, she was with some other girls, holding hands and singing as they went around in a circle. It looked like fun, so I said, "Dorothy, can I play?" But I must have said her name wrong, because she got mad.

"Are you talking to me?" she said. She put her hands on her hips and leaned forward. "There is no 'Dorzee' here. So go away, why don't you? Go away until you learn to talk right. You can go right back to where you came from for all I care."

I knew then there was no point in asking her again.

Besides, it was Lydia I wanted for a friend. Lydia knew how to speak English. She understood everything.

And she had store-bought clothes with barrettes and hair bands that matched. My clothes were nice too, because Tati made them himself, but sometimes I wished they looked like the clothes the other kids wore.

I thought Lydia was really lucky. It didn't occur to me that her family might have troubles too, until the day I overheard Mrs. Sniderman and Mami talking.

It was a warm evening in May. They were on the porch, Mami drinking tea, Mrs. Sniderman sipping from a bottle of Pepsi. Lydia and I were sitting in a puddle of light on the pavement playing jacks.

"The man is dead now," I heard Mrs. Sniderman say. "He was Italian man, but he was living in Canada long time. Before the war even. He goes with the Canada army to fight. The mother is not Italian. She is Hungarian, or maybe Romanian. I not remember."

At first I couldn't figure out who Mrs. Sniderman was talking about, and I kept my eyes on Lydia, because I knew Mami would end the conversation if she thought I was listening.

Lydia grabbed for three jacks with each bounce of the tiny red ball as Mrs. Sniderman said, "The woman has no family. She comes to Canada after the war. She is war bride. Already she has the baby when she comes. The man, he work hard. After the war he had good job. He work for the city. He work to build the subway.

Good pay. They buy nice house. Then, three years ago, *pfuuut!* The man gets hurt. His leg was broken. And here"—she put her hand on her back—"here is bad. He not lifting nothing no more. The subway job is finish. He cannot work. They not want him."

"They had a house?" I could tell Mami was impressed. A house was something she dreamed of. "But how did he die?"

"When the subway job is no more, he goes to work in the chicken-killing place where big trucks bring the chickens from the farm. There is big storm, and there is wind and rain. Much lightning. The truck comes back, back, back to the wall where the man is standing. The driver, he does not see. There is noise from the thunder. The man, he is pushed to the wall."

She clapped loudly. "*Platsch!*" she said.

I gasped, distracting Lydia. When she missed the ball, I reached for it.

On the porch, Mami said, "What a terrible death!"

The ball slipped through my fingers too.

"We're both butterfingers." Lydia chuckled as she leaned forward to gather the jacks.

Mrs. Sniderman continued. "Oh, he does not die right away. He is in the hospital first. Long time. Long, long time. Lots and lots of money it costs. *Then* he dies."

I was trying so hard to think about who she was talking about that I couldn't think to move.

"Theresa. Throw!" Lydia said again.

The jacks tumbled from my fingers.

"The woman has to sell the house to pay," Mrs. Sniderman said. "Then there is no more money. His family will not help. They say the girl belongs not to him."

"That poor woman," Mami said. "That poor little girl."

"Poor, yes." Mrs. Sniderman nodded her agreement. "And now they are living in one room on Kensington Avenue."

"Such a pity." Mami sighed. "No father. No family."

No father. No family. Lydia? Was she talking about Lydia? Lydia's father died such a horrible death?

"Theresa?" Lydia said.

I lifted my head. Saw her frown. She turned to look at the porch. "What's that old lady talking about?"

I shrugged. "She...she was talking Yiddish," I whispered, as if that answered the question.

"Stupid Tepsi!" Lydia scooped up the jacks and dropped them into a small cloth bag. "I'm going home."

Stupid?

Lydia stood and ran across the street. I watched her go. I didn't want to stop her anyway.

Twenty

When I stepped outside the next morning, Mrs. Sniderman was standing behind a wooden table piled with tea towels, tablecloths, linens and pillowcases. Brightly patterned housedresses waved like flags from a rack beside the sidewalk. "Is best quality. You like?" I heard her say to a woman who was leaning down to examine a lace doily. I didn't hear what the woman answered, because Lydia came out just then, and I hurried across the street. "Our grass has a store," I said.

She nodded. "Yeah. Just wait. When the good weather comes, the market will stretch all the way down the street, and your Tepsi lady won't be the only one with a store on her lawn."

I frowned. "Why are you calling Mrs. Sniderman Tepsi?"

"Everybody does. It's 'cause she drinks Pepsi Cola all the time and she can't say the name right. She says Tepsi Cola."

She giggled then, and I might have joined her, but I remembered how bad I felt about calling the Little Man "Buzzard," and I began to wonder if the things *I* said wrong made Lydia laugh too.

My mind was filled with thoughts like that as we walked down Dundas Street, so I didn't say anything, and it wasn't until we stopped for the lights at the corner of Spadina Avenue that Lydia said, "Your mom goes to work every day now, eh?"

"Yes, every day. She goes to a different house. She cleans for ladies that have much money."

The lights changed, and we started across.

"What a lousy job!" Lydia said.

"Lousy?"

"Crummy. Like, not good," she explained.

I heard, but I didn't know what to say, because it felt as if she was saying something bad about my mother.

"Where does *your* mother work?" I asked when we reached the other side.

Lydia kicked at a pebble, ran after it, kicked it again before she called back. "She works in a big office building downtown."

"What does she do?"

She kicked the pebble back into my path as if she was inviting me to take a turn before she said, "She cleans the offices."

"Cleaning offices...is not lousy job?"

"Do you know how rich you have to be to have an office in one of those buildings?"

I didn't know how to answer that, but when I reached the pebble, I kicked it into the street, hard. "Your mother, she is working late," I pointed out.

"Yeah. So? You can't clean offices in the middle of the day. You have to wait till people go home."

"When is she coming home?"

"Way after midnight. Except when they make her work an extra shift. Then she doesn't come till morning."

I thought about this office cleaning job. It didn't sound all that good to me. "Are you...scary?" I asked.

"Scared? Why should I be scared?"

"I mean...alone...in the dark?"

"I'm not scared," she said quickly. But after a while she added, "Only if there's thunder and lightning. I hate thunderstorms. Are you? Scared of the dark, I mean?"

"I am not baby," I said, as if that answered her question.

"Come on, I'll race you to school!" she called as she took off running.

"No fair!" I shouted, but I followed her around the corner of Beverly Street, and we didn't stop until we reached the schoolyard.

—◈—

"English and German have lots of words the same, you know," I told Mami as I cleaned carrots for our dinner.

"Really? What words?"

"Lousy and *lausig*. They sound the same, don't they?"

"Do they mean the same?"

"I think so." After a bit I said, "Do you like your job?"

She glanced at me. "Like it? It's not a job to like. It's a pay-for-food-and-rent job." She waved me aside. "Get out of the way," she said as she lifted the pot filled with water and potatoes to the stove.

I stepped aside and stood with my back to the wall.

My mother said "Get out of the way" every time she had to light the stove. She was afraid of it. I could tell. She worried that it might explode, like the bombs she remembered from the war.

The stove was old, and mostly black, but it had a white enameled oven door. Patches of the enamel were missing, so it had the spotted look of the cows that lived on the farm in Austria where we used to buy milk.

Mami was always saying, "Don't go near the stove!" And she never, ever let me cook anything, even when she was standing right beside me.

From my side of the room, I watched her lean forward to turn a handle. There was a loud *sssssssssss*, followed by the smell of gas. A match flared, and she held it toward the element.

Sometimes the gas popped right away and blue flames danced in a bright circle. This time the *sssssssssss* went on and on and on. My nose quivered at the smell of escaping gas. I held my breath. Mami's hand began to shake. She bent from her middle and backed away, so only her arm and the hand holding the flaming match stayed near the ring.

Finally there was a loud *POP*, followed by a flash of fire that made us both gasp and jump.

"Lousy stove!" I said.

Mami made a sound of agreement. She moved the pot over the burning ring, then came to the table and sagged into a chair. She looked tired. Maybe Lydia was right. Maybe cleaning houses was a lousy job.

"Is it better here?" I asked. "Better than home?"

"Better? I don't have to carry water or chop wood. But look." She lifted the hem of her skirt to show the bruises on her knees. "This week three ladies wanted the wax stripped from the bedroom floors. Three days on my knees, scrubbing. Is it better in Canada? Not better. Just different."

She sat up, and her tone changed. "But for you it will be better. You can go to school, and you won't have to be a cleaning lady."

"And I won't have a lousy gas stove either," I said.

Twenty-One

One night, when the house was dark, we heard noises in the sunroom: soft swishing sounds; scratching, scraping, rustling sounds; and then a soft *THUD*.

"What was that?" Mami whispered.

Tati groaned and climbed out of bed. His footsteps padded through the kitchen. Then…silence.

"What are you doing?" Mami called.

"Listening."

"Do you hear anything?"

"No."

His footsteps padded back.

"Well, aren't you going to do anything?"

"What do you want me to do? It's dark."

Bedsprings squeaked. More silence. Eventually I slept.

It was Mami who discovered what was making the sounds in the sunroom. "Look at this!" she said, waving a carrot at my father when he came home from work the next day. "Look at those marks. They're too big for mice. You know what that means."

"What? What does it mean?" I asked.

She walked to the sink, turning her back to me.

"Well? What does it mean? Why doesn't anybody ever answer my questions?"

"It's a rat!" Mami said. "Are you happy? Now you know. It's a rat! I hate rats."

"Me too," I said, but I couldn't help thinking how funny it was that we had a rat in our sunroom now. And I hadn't seen a single one on the boat coming over here.

All through dinner Mami grumbled about the rat. She complained again the next day and the day after that.

We kept the sunroom door closed, but now that we knew what was making the sounds, we seemed to hear them more often.

"There," Mami whispered one night. "Did you hear that? I can't sleep with that creature outside our door."

"If you keep talking, nobody else will sleep either," Tati grumbled.

Her complaints got louder. "For all we know, it's a female. There'll be a family in no time. We'll have rats running over our beds at night. We'll have rats chewing on our ears and noses!"

I shuddered at the thought. "How big is it?" I wanted to know.

"Who knows?" she said. "Rats come in different sizes. At home they were big. Your father saw one attack a small dog once. He won't tell you, but I know it bit into the dog's throat and wouldn't let go. Someone had to hit it with a stick to get it off, and the dog died anyway."

I cringed. No wonder Tati didn't want to deal with our rat.

I began dreaming about rats. In one dream a large rat sat on my chest, cleaning its whiskers. It lifted its chin and combed its long nails through the gray fur of its belly. When it turned to me, its eyes glowed red. "I always wash before dinner," it said. Dinner, I realized, would be me.

"TATI!" I screamed. I woke to find my father bending over me.

"It was going to eat me," I gasped.

"Shhh," he said. "You'll wake everybody. What was going to eat you?"

"The rat. It was on my chest."

"There!" Mami said. "What did I tell you? You need to get rid of the rat."

"You need to stop talking about it. It's all your talk that's scaring her. If you keep this up, none of us will sleep." He leaned over to tuck in my sheets.

But Mami wasn't done. "Oh, so now it's my fault," she said. "We wouldn't have a problem if you just got rid of it.

Tati didn't say anything as he climbed back into bed, and for the next few days the house stayed quiet.

And then, on a Monday evening—I know it was a Monday because Mami was on her way through the sunroom to hang laundry on the garden lines—the rat darted across her path. That evening my mother stopped complaining and started shouting. "If that rat stays, I'm not going through that sunroom ever again. Get rid of the rat, or *you* can hang out the laundry."

"Don't threaten me!" Tati shouted. His fingers raked through his hair, and the little bump at the side of his forehead started to bounce. I could see how mad he was, but it didn't stop my mother.

"You're the man in this family. This is your job. Do it, or take over mine!"

Tati's face turned redder.

"Fine!" he shouted. "If that's what it takes to bring peace into this house, I'll get rid of the rat." He stomped out of the kitchen, slamming the sunroom door and making the windows rattle. We heard the door to the yard opening.

"Will the rat run away?" I asked.

"If it does, it will only come back," Mami said.

The rat must have stayed, because Tati started moving things out.

That sunroom was full of stuff. We used it to store our bucket and some rags, a broom and dustpan, a yellow dust mop and my brown galoshes. There was a basket with potatoes and carrots and a cabbage, all nibbled on by the rat.

Mrs. Sniderman used the space to store things too. When I heard grunting noises, I knew Tati was dragging out the old mattress, the wooden storm windows, the rusty baby carriage and empty picture frames.

"There you are," we heard him say. "There's no point in hiding. There aren't many hiding places left." And we knew he was talking to the rat.

His words made Mami groan. "He doesn't have anything to kill it with," she said, reaching for the door. But she didn't open it, because right then we heard a sharp "AHH!" followed by a loud *THUMP!* The sounds continued in a steady rhythm. "AHH!" *THUMP! THUMP! THUMP!* "AHH!" *THUMP! THUMP! THUMP!*

Then there was silence.

"Adam?" Mami called.

"I'm all right," he said.

When we opened the door, we found my father wiping sweat from his forehead with the back of one hand and holding the dust mop in the other. His breath was loud, as if he had been running. The rat lay at his feet.

"It attacked the mop," he said. "Bit into the fuzzy part…wouldn't let go. Look at it…still attached. I had to…had to pound it…to death."

"Take it outside," Mami said in the same tone she might say "Take out the garbage."

Tati dragged out the rat before he shook it free from the mop. We helped him carry everything back inside.

When we were done, Mami said, "Go. Your father has to wash." And Tati took off his shirt so he could wash up at the kitchen sink while I went to find Lydia.

"Come on," I said as we ran across the street giggling nervously. "You can see it. It's dead. It's just lying there, in our backyard."

In the growing darkness we slipped around the garbage cans and through the narrow space between our house and the neighbors'. We paused at the rickety gate before we walked into the backyard, slowly, solemnly, to stare at death. The rat lay stretched on the ground. It was long and large and sleek. Its gray coat was only slightly matted. It wasn't as big as a small dog, but it was big enough.

"Eew! Look at his teeth," Lydia said. "Look how long they are."

I stared at the threads of yellow fuzz stuck between the orange teeth. We both took a step back. The rat was dead, but even in death it looked dangerous, as if it might, without warning, leap to its feet. The danger lay in the staring eyes, the long teeth, even in the blood clotted around the nostrils. I knew then that it had taken a lot of courage for Tati to kill the rat, and I was relieved to have a father brave enough to do the job.

Twenty-Two

The schoolyard was abuzz with excitement.

"Last day."

"No more teachers, no more books."

"Summer holidays."

Everybody was smiling and happy. Everybody except me. I wasn't sure how I felt about summer holidays. What would I do when I didn't have school to go to every day?

When the morning recess bell rang, Miss Lamb had everybody line up, but she told Roberto and me to stay behind. "I need to talk to you," she said.

"Somebody's in trouble," Dorothy sang as she slid out of her chair.

Trouble? The word thudded into my head. Trouble? My chest tightened. It hurt to breathe. I didn't want to be in trouble. I glanced at Roberto. He shrugged. No help at all.

Miss Lamb walked the class out. We waited. The room felt heavy with silence. On the wall the clock *tock, tock, tocked* out the seconds. Surely it was never that loud before? I sighed, picked at the skin beside my thumbnail, tried to breathe.

When she came back, Miss Lamb pulled two chairs to her desk. "Come," she said. "Sit here with me."

She didn't sound angry, but the word *trouble* kept a steady beat in my head. I sucked air through my teeth. Roberto squirmed. It didn't help.

"You're not in trouble," Miss Lamb said kindly. She pushed her beautiful hair behind her ear as we waited to hear what she had to say. "I want to talk to you about your report cards."

Report cards? I tried to think what "report cards" might mean.

"Your report cards…," she began. "I know how hard you've worked…how much you've learned. But I have to mark you for what you *can* do, and I'm afraid when I give you your report cards, you'll be disappointed. Not happy," she added.

She pulled two envelopes from her desk drawer

and handed them to us. "I want you to look at them now, before the class comes back, in case you have questions."

I opened the flap, pulled out the small square card inside. My name was printed on the front. *Theresa Marie Becker*. Inside was some writing and the letters *D, D, A, D, D*.

Then I knew. In Austria report cards had numbers. Ones and twos and threes and fours, with ones being the best. My old report cards were full of ones. I stared at the letters on this card. The *A* was for arithmetic. Grade-three arithmetic. And the *D*s? I felt my shoulders sag. The pain in my chest grew.

Miss Lamb said something about grade four. "You didn't fail," she said.

Didn't fail? I wanted to tell her I should be going into grade six.

"Do you have any questions?"

I looked down. What was there to ask? Could I ask her why no magic happened for me? Why I didn't learn as much as I needed to know? Why learning English took so long and was so much harder than I thought?

"Is there something you want to know?" she asked again.

I glanced at Roberto. We shook our heads.

"Then you may go."

We walked down the hall. "Maybe I will be in trouble," I said when we reached the door. "You?"

He shrugged and ran off to the boy's side of the yard.

~🙢~

Supper was over before I found the courage to hand over my report card. Tati studied it, handed it to Mami. She looked at it. I waited. The weight in my chest sat boulder-heavy.

"The magic didn't happen for me," I said, trying to explain the low marks.

"Magic?" Tati said.

"Mami said I would learn to speak English like magic, but no magic happened."

"Magic?" Mami's voice was shrill. "Magic doesn't happen by itself. You have to help it along! Did you do that? Did you listen? Did you learn? Did you do your best?"

"Miss Lamb said I did my best."

"So," Tati said. "Next year will be a new start. And you'll keep doing your best so we don't see any more of these *D*s, right, Mouse?"

I nodded. The boulder shifted, but it didn't go away.

~🙢~

That evening things only got worse. Mami showed me the letter I had written to the Besselmeyers. It had come back marked: *RETURN TO SENDER*. "I guess they left," she said.

"Left the lager?" I asked. "What about Martin? Did he go too? How will we find them?

"The world is a much smaller place than you think, Theresa," Tati said. "People don't stay lost forever. I'm sure we'll hear sooner or later."

"Children stay lost!" I blurted. "Mami told me. She said children get lost. Aunt Theresa's children did. And nobody ever found them."

A look of pain crossed Tati's face. "Write your letter, Mouse," he said. "I'll buy you a stamp."

So I wrote to Martin and waited to hear back.

In the morning I thought I could sleep in. "Summer holidays," I mumbled when Mami woke me.

"Holidays? I don't have holidays," she said. "I have to go to work. Get up. I want to see you combed and dressed and fed before I'm gone."

So, just like every other day, I got up before seven. At eight Mami left, and I was alone. Holidays, I thought. Oh well. With the market right up the street, there had to be something to do on Kensington Avenue.

Twenty-Three

Mami started every morning with a long list of rules. "Make the beds and tidy up before you go outside. Don't spend the day running in and out—you'll annoy Mrs. Sniderman. You are not to bother her. Understand?"

I nodded.

"And stay away from the stove. Don't touch it." She glanced my way. "Are you listening?"

I took a sip of tea and nodded again.

While she leaned over the kitchen sink to brush her teeth, I nibbled my toast. She rinsed and wiped away spatters before she went on. "Don't go off the street and don't bring anyone into the house when we're not home. Be careful. Keep the door locked."

She slid my key across the table. "Here, don't forget this."

I picked it up, slipped the blue ribbon around my neck and clutched the key in my hand to warm it before I let it fall inside my blouse.

"Don't talk to strangers," she went on as she buttoned her sweater. "Eat all your lunch. It's in the icebox. Behave yourself," she finished, leaning down to kiss my cheek.

"Mami…," I began.

"What?" She sounded wary.

The words *Stay home* were on my tongue. But one look at the tight lines around her mouth stopped me. We both knew there was no point. She *had* to go to work. I *had* to stay home.

"See you tonight," I said.

She sighed; then she was gone.

The morning list of rules was long, and every so often it grew longer when something new was added. "Don't take our blankets outside" was added after one perfect day when Lydia came over to play and we used my blanket to build a tent in our backyard. We were pretending to be desert princesses. Then our evil uncle, the magician, became part of the story.

"We have to escape," Lydia announced, "or he'll turn us into toads." Of course we ran out of the yard. What else could we do? We ran crisscross through the market streets, hiding from our imaginary uncle until we reached the butcher shop.

"Look! Look!" I whispered in my terrified princess voice as I pointed at the shaved pink head of the pig displayed in the shop window. The pig stared blindly into the street. Long pale lashes fanned its dead eyes. "He's turned our brother into a pig and killed him," I said. We gasped in pretend terror and ran around another corner as our game continued.

I forgot about the blanket, and Mami came home to find it sagging in the dirt. She used the wooden spoon that day, and I had to kneel in the corner while she washed and hung the blanket on the line to dry. I really didn't need new reminders, but once a rule was added to the list, it stayed.

One morning I sat quietly while Mami went through the list. I sat while she picked up her purse and walked through the bedroom. I waited until she walked out the door, but as soon as she was gone, I got ready to go too. There was no point in staying in an empty kitchen. I walked out, leaving the dirty dishes and the unmade beds. I could ignore Mami's voice repeating the morning instructions, but I couldn't ignore the silence in the house. It swirled around me, rang in my ears, pressed on my chest. There was nothing to do but go.

I would come back to do my chores when the house was awake: when Mrs. Sniderman moved in her room, when the Little Man shuffled about upstairs, when the house was filled with sunshine. Things were always tidy by the time Mami came home; they just didn't get done in the morning.

I wandered up Kensington Avenue to where people were getting ready for the day. The air was morning-cool, but the sun was bright with the promise of another hot day. The market vendors were hosing down sidewalks, filling the street with a dark, earthy smell that competed with the aroma of the bread from the bakery and the sharp bite from barrels of murky brine that held herring or pickles or peppers.

I was standing at the fish store, watching the shadows of silver-finned fish circling a galvanized tank, when something brushed my leg. The touch startled me, and I turned to see a brown and orange cat slipping around the sidewalk displays. "*Mitz, Mitz, Mitz*," I called. The cat didn't pause.

A Canadian cat, I thought. How do you call a Canadian cat?

The cat skirted boxes and baskets arranged along the edge of the sidewalk before it slipped into an alley between two stalls. Without thinking, I followed.

The alley opened to a small backyard filled with piles of weathered crates and towering stacks of bushel baskets. In the far corner stood a rotting shed. Grayed by years of wind and weather, it sagged against an equally ancient fence. I stopped, my eyes searching for the cat. When I saw a flash of color between that shed and the fence, I called, "*Mitz! Mitz! Mitz!*" I was sure there was an answering *Meow*.

The space the cat had slipped through was narrow and piled with old boards that shifted under my feet, but they weren't going to stop me. Not when I was so close. Bracing myself against the shed, I slip-stepped along until I reached the end of the wall. It was tight, but I managed to put my head around the corner.

Then I saw them. Four furry bundles wobbling from a ragged opening at the bottom of the shed. Kittens. They were small and fuzzy. All I wanted to do was play with them.

"*Mitz, Mitz, Mitz*," I called. The mother arched her back, raised her fur and hissed a warning.

I gasped. Face to face, the cat was not pretty. She looked painfully thin, and the fur that wasn't standing on end was matted. She only had one good eye. The other one had an empty socket that oozed pus.

I pulled back, but with my head around the corner, I couldn't leave easily.

A memory of Martin facing a barnyard dog flashed into my mind.

"Never show fear," he had said as the dog bounded toward us. I remembered how he made me stand still, how he stretched out his hand, how the dog stopped barking and sniffed, then wagged his tail and played with us.

"*Mitz, Mitz, Mitz,*" I whispered, stretching my hand out. The cat flew at me. As her claws raked my arm, I cried out and jerked back, ramming my head and elbow into the fence. The wood under my feet shifted. I fell forward, smacking my chin into the shed, and then back again, cracking my head on a post. My elbows and both knees scraped painfully against the rough boards as I stumbled out.

Terrified that the hissing cat was right behind me, I ran through the yard, out of the alley and down the street toward home. My breath came in short, sharp gasps as I struggled to hold back tears. I didn't want to cry. Not in the street where anybody could see. But as soon as I walked into the house, my stifled sobs burst free.

"Stupid, stupid, stupid!" I cried as I tried to fit my key into the lock. But blinded by tears, I couldn't see. I slumped to sit on the bottom step, where I cried some more.

It was during a gasp between sobs that I heard a papery voice say, "Sarah?"

I looked up. The Little Man was on the stairs, clutching the railing. He was making his way down, one step at a time. He's afraid of falling, I thought, swallowing my tears.

When he was four steps down, he stopped and pointed at Mrs. Sniderman's door, "Knock," he wheezed.

I knocked, but Mrs. Sniderman didn't answer. I knew she wouldn't. It was such a nice day, she would have set up her store outside if she was home.

The Little Man beckoned. "Come," he said. I heard his breath rattling in his chest as he climbed back up. At the top he braced his elbows on the railing and stood, panting. Then he slippered into his room.

With all of Mami's warnings about strangers echoing in my head, I stayed in the hallway until he came out again, holding what looked like a faded piece of flannel and a bar of soap. When he waved me upstairs, I decided that the Little Man had only ever been kind to me, so I went.

In the bathroom he let the water run warm before he wet the cloth and soaped it. I watched him lower himself to sit on the edge of the tub.

"Come," he said, reaching for me.

I stepped forward, my lips tight, and stretched out my hand. He looked at my arm, splotched red and marked with three angry lines sprouting pinhead bubbles of blood.

"Cat?" he asked.

I nodded.

He shook his head. Wheezed. Ran the cloth up and down my arm.

If Mami had scrubbed as firmly, I would have cried and fussed, but I stayed silent as the Little Man washed the dirt and blood from my arm, my chin, my elbows and my knees. How could I complain when I could see how hard this was for him?

"There," he said when he was done. "Best to let air dry."

I nodded.

"I'm Theresa," I said, thinking to let him know my real name.

The Little Man said nothing. "My mother's name is Leni and my father is Adam," I went on. "What's your name?"

"Adam?" he said. It sounded like a question.

"My tati is Adam," I explained, thinking that my English wasn't clear. "What's your name?"

"Adam?" the Little Man said again.

"You're Adam too?"

A thin smile flitted across his face. Then he waved his hand at me to go. I thanked him and left.

For the rest of the day I stayed close to home, my stomach in knots. What would Mami say when she found out how many rules I had broken?

It was raining when Mami walked through the door. She was soaked. Even so, she noticed right away that something was wrong.

"What have you been up to?" she asked as she peeled off her wet clothing and hung it on the line that stretched across the sunroom.

I sighed and told her about the cat. When I got to the part about the Little Man, she looked at me. I talked faster, hoping she wouldn't think to ask questions.

"He washed the dirt away with soap and warm water. That was nice of him, wasn't it? He told me the air would be better for the scratches than bandages, but I don't think he had any bandages anyway."

She reached for my arm and examined the scratches. "Cat scratches can cause all kinds of problems," she said.

I pulled away. "Did you know that his name is Adam too?" I said, hoping to change the subject. It didn't work.

"Where was this cat?" she asked.

"Just up the street," I lied, remembering the *Don't go off the street* rule.

Her eyes narrowed. "Theresa," she said, "you know it's a sin to tell a lie and an even bigger sin to disobey your mother."

I squirmed. My stomach dropped. "I know."

Outside, lightning flashed, brightening the room. The light was followed by a heavy rumble of thunder. It reminded me of a story Mami told when I was small. *Lightning and thunder are signs that God is angry*, she had said. *God hates lies. He punishes liars.* I felt sick.

"Mami," I said, preparing to tell her that I had gone off the street.

"Did he touch you anywhere else?" she asked.

"What? Oh, no!" I was relieved that this answer was a truthful one. "He's a nice man. Really. You said a man that doesn't like children is not to be trusted, but the Little Man likes me. He calls me Sarah."

"Ha!" Mami flashed back. "He doesn't even know your name. He may be nice, and he may be related to Mrs. Sniderman, but as far as you're concerned he's a stranger. Make sure you stay away from him from now on."

Tears filled my eyes.

"Look at me, Theresa," she said, lifting my chin and staring into my face. "Are you telling me the truth?"

"Yes!" I said, the tears overflowing. But I wasn't sure which truth she was asking about.

Another brilliant flash lit up the kitchen, followed by a window-rattling crash. I gasped. Mami crossed herself quickly.

"I...I...," I started, prepared to tell everything before it was too late, but Mami turned to the sink, and the sounds of the wind and rain and the running water drowned my words.

After supper, Tati and I went upstairs to thank the Little Man for helping me. We knocked on his door and waited. There was a shuffling sound inside, but the door stayed closed.

"That's odd," Mami said when we came back. "And I seem to remember that Mrs. Sniderman said his name is Aaron or Avrum or something like that. Why would he tell you his name is Adam?"

The next day, two new "Don'ts" were added to my mother's morning list: *Don't play with the market cats*, and *Don't bother the Little Man*.

She didn't need to worry about the market cats. I never wanted to make friends with any of them again. And I didn't want to bother the Little Man. But I saw him every day: in the hallway, on the stairs, in the market. And I still ate the caramels he left on the newel posts. They were too good to pass up.

Twenty-Four

One day Mami came home from work late. "I'm so tired. There was an accident on Queen Street, and we sat on the streetcar for almost an hour," she said. "I need you to run to the store and get me a loaf of rye bread, a small bottle of milk and a package of chicken noodle soup. I have to make supper in a hurry." She handed me a two-dollar bill from her purse. "Don't forget to count the change," she called as I hurried up the street.

I went from one store to the next, buying bread at the bakery and milk at the dairy before I went into the small grocery store. It was the hardest place to shop, not because I didn't know how to ask for Lipton Chicken Noodle Soup, but because the shopkeeper always served grown-ups first. It didn't matter how long I waited, if a new grown-up came in, I had to wait.

When I finally had the soup, I hurried home, but I knew as soon as I walked into the kitchen that something was wrong. There were no cooking noises, no dinner smells, and strangest of all, Mami was sitting on a chair, staring into the room. Her arms were folded across her middle and she was rocking back and forth. I had never seen her do that before. "Are you sick?" I asked.

No answer.

Then I saw it. On the table beside her lay a letter, one blue page, tissue thin, and beside it a small picture of the Virgin Mary. The picture had a black frame. I knew what that meant. "Who died?" I asked.

"We should have stayed," Mami said. "We should have stayed." Her mouth opened, and I thought she was going to scream, but the scream stayed in her throat, and all that came out was a tight moan.

"Oma? Is it Oma?"

She nodded and lifted her apron to cover her face. Still rocking, she began to sob. "She didn't want to die alone."

I stood, watching, not sure what to say or do. Eventually Mami let the apron fall and tugged a handkerchief from her pocket to blow her nose. Then she pulled me to her lap. She wrapped her arms around me and we sat together, crying for Oma, who died alone.

After supper my parents said they were going to church to ask Father Kelly to say a mass for Oma's soul. "You'll have to stay by yourself for a while," Tati said, and I could tell from his voice there was no point complaining.

As usual, Mami gave me instructions as she was getting ready to go.

"Don't forget to sweep the floor when the dishes are done. Make sure you stay inside. I don't want you playing in the street in the evening when we're not home. Don't open the door for anyone." Then she put her hand on my shoulder. "We won't be long," she said. "And Mrs. Sniderman's home. You won't be alone."

With nothing else to do, I washed the dishes and swept the floor. When I was done, I slipped the gnome's eye under my pillow and climbed into bed with Lissi and a book. I read as the sky outside turned gray, then black. By that time my eyes burned with tiredness. I wanted to sleep, but I was afraid to get out of bed to turn off the light. You're being silly, I told myself. You're not a baby. Turn off the light.

Finally, clutching the gnome's eye in one hand, I bounded out of bed, flicked off the light and leaped back. I pulled my sheet over my head and squeezed my eyes shut.

You're not alone, I told myself. You're not alone.
Mrs. Sniderman is on the other side of the wall. There
are people upstairs.

But out of the darkness came a scrabbling sound
in the wall, a scuttling in the basement, a creak on the
stairs, a scritching in the kitchen. I held my breath,
listening. For a while there was silence; then the
kitchen sounds began again. *Scritch-scritch. Scritch-
scritch. Scritch-scritch.*

Mice, I thought. Just mice in the cupboard. I let
my breath out slowly so as not to disturb the night.

Upstairs the *schlup-schlup, schlup-schlup, schlup-
schlup* sounds of the Little Man's footsteps began. As
I listened, my heartbeat slowed to match his familiar
rhythm.

From the other side of the wall, I heard Mrs.
Sniderman's long, slow sleeping whistle. *Swhooooo.
Swhooooo.* If my parents were home, I'd be asleep too,
I thought.

*Schlup-schlup, schlup-schlup, swhooooo. Schlup-
schlup, schlup-schlup, swhooooo.*

⁓❦◦

I was surprised to see the train pull into the station.
The iron wheels slowed, then stopped.

"Go," Mami said. "Go and see."

"Yes, go," Tati said, lifting his chin in the direction of the platform.

I stood, undecided, curious to see who was coming but afraid to find out.

A cloud of steam escaped from behind the engine. I whirled, straining for a glimpse of...something... anything. Where was everybody?

"Mami?"

But it wasn't Mami who stepped out of the engine's mist. It was a hunched figure dressed in long black skirts. She came floating toward me. Gnarled fingers clutched the knitted shawl to her chest. A dark kerchief shadowed her face.

"Oma...? Oma?"

Yes, I was sure. "Mami!" I called into the fog. "Look, Mami, it's Oma! She's not dead. She's right here."

There was no answer. I turned back. "We thought you died," I began.

Oma ignored my words. "Your hair is still red," she said. "There are no redheads in our family. Heaven only knows where *you* came from."

Tears filled my eyes.

"Say something!" she said. "Speak up."

My throat closed, and I knew I couldn't speak without crying.

"For goodness sake, Mouse. You can't cry about

every little thing." It was Tati's voice. He sounded annoyed.

"I never told lies when I was her age," Mami said.

The tears overflowed. I tried to wipe them away so Tati wouldn't scold.

"Where's your gnome's eye?" a voice asked.

"Martin?" I whipped around, straining to see through the mist.

"Martin?"

He began to chant: "Oma has red hair! Oma has red hair!"

"It's white! It's white! Nobody in our family has red hair!" Oma screeched.

"Oma has red hair!" Martin's voice sang again.

"You lie! You lie! My hair is white!"

And then I did a terrible thing. I reached up, and with one quick jerk I pulled Oma's kerchief down.

Her hair wasn't white. It *was* red: thick and bright and shiny. Redder than mine. And, as I watched, it changed from hair to flames that flickered in the dim light.

She turned to me. I thought she would be angry, but her face looked sad. "Start telling the truth," she said. "God punishes liars."

The flames became hair again, red hair like mine, and she began to shrink. She got smaller and smaller, and then, just like in a fairy tale, she disappeared.

"Did you see? Did you see?" I said.

"See what?" Mami asked. I opened my eyes. She was adjusting my blanket. "Go back to sleep," she said. "Go back to sleep."

But I didn't sleep. I felt hot, and my head ached. My throat felt raw and sore, as if I was trying to swallow ground glass. "Mami," I whimpered. "Mami, I think I'm sick."

Twenty-Five

Mami made chamomile tea with lemon and honey. She soaked rags in vinegar and water and wrapped them around my wrists, my ankles, my neck and across my forehead. She sat by my bed and watched over me while I slept. When I woke, I lay, limp and groggy, listening to her worried whispers coming from the kitchen.

"What should I do? Theresa's still sick. I should stay home." She made a small moaning sound before she added, "If I do, I could lose the job."

"Go to work," I heard Tati say. "Theresa can take care of herself. You said yourself her fever's gone."

"You always think she can take care of herself."

"I was cutting my own bread…"

"...by the time you were three," Mami finished for him.

"Well, I was. Our mother never fussed over us the way you do over Theresa, and we all grew up fine."

"You didn't grow up in a city filled with strangers!"

Hearing the worry in Mami's voice, I slipped out of bed and padded toward the kitchen. "It's okay if you go," I said. "I'll be all right."

She wavered. "Promise you'll stay at home," she said. "I don't want your fever to come back."

I nodded.

"Promise," she said again.

"I promise," I said, climbing back into bed.

That morning I read and dozed and read some more. For a while I pretended my bed was the sea. I told Lissi stories about Herman-the-Pest, and rats and whales. When I heard Mrs. Sniderman humming, I closed my eyes and listened. I'm not a mouse, I told myself. I'm not scared.

Then a door opened, and Mrs. Sniderman left. Friday, I remembered. She visits her daughter on Fridays. A fist in my chest clenched until the familiar *schlup-schlup* sounds of the Little Man's feet slippered along the upper hallway. Not alone. Not alone. Not alone, I told myself. I closed my eyes and dozed again until his shuffling steps started down the stairs.

"Don't go! Don't go! Don't go!" I whispered, but when the front door opened and then closed, a wave of panic washed over me.

Promise you'll stay home, Mami had said. *Promise.* And I had promised. But that was then...Now? Now I decided the front porch counted as home. Why would Mami mind if I sat in the sunshine?

Hurrying into my clothes, I grabbed Lissi and went out to sit on the porch bench. Lydia saw me and came over. "I'll get my doll, and we'll play," she said. She ran home, and I waited.

As the noon sun beamed down, I shifted into the shadow of the porch. The street was empty. The only sounds came from an open window next door, where radio voices sang about a dog in a window, and from the trees, where something shrilled a high-pitched sound. I must have dozed again, because I jumped when Lydia said, "Sorry, I had to stay and eat lunch."

"It's okay," I said, squinting at the doll she was holding. I groped for Lissi. She wasn't on my lap. I looked around. She wasn't on the bench or on the porch. She wasn't on the ground nearby. My beautiful red-haired baby doll was gone.

"Who else was here?" Lydia asked.

"Nobody. There was nobody. I was by myself."

"Except the Buzzard."

"The Little Man? He went out."

"He came back."

"He did?"

"He just went in. I saw him. I bet he took it."

"Why would he take my doll?"

"He's all the time carrying that big bag around. I bet he steals lots of stuff. I just betcha. Besides, there was nobody else, was there?"

"I don't think…," I said. But of course I didn't know.

After that I didn't want to play. I went back inside. The Little Man *was* home. I could hear the *schlup-schlup* sound of his pacing, and a soft droning sound. Was he singing? I thought about going upstairs and knocking. Thought about saying, "Did you take my doll?" Thought about how silly that sounded. And I remembered Mami's warning: *Don't bother the Little Man.*

What could I do? I had never felt more miserable. If I wasn't such a mouse, I would have stayed inside. Now Lissi was lost, my mother would know that I broke my promise, and worse, the Besselmeyers would be sad if they ever found out I hadn't taken care of their gift.

By the time Mami came home, my pillow was damp with tears. She gasped when she saw me. "You're feeling worse," she said. "I knew I should have stayed."

I shook my head. "This was all my fault," I sobbed, and I told her the whole story and waited to be punished.

She didn't do anything. Nothing. Nothing at all. She didn't even yell. Somehow that made me feel worse.

Only one good thing happened that day. Onkel Johann stopped by after supper. "I have a surprise for you," he said pulling a letter from his jacket pocket.

"It's from Frau Besselmeyer," Tati said, looking at the envelope. He opened it, then read aloud.

"*I have been praying you all got to Canada safely. If you found Johann, then I know you're in good hands, because he is a good man.*"

We all smiled at Onkel Johann, and his own smile stretched across his face as Tati read on.

"*After you left, Thomas was moved into a sanitarium because of his cough. He is already feeling better. Everything worked out so well. I got a job in the same hospital, taking care of children who have TB. I help them wash and dress and make sure they eat well. It is good to be surrounded by young people when you are getting old.*"

"A children's home is the perfect place for her," Mami said. "She is such a kind woman." She sighed then, and I knew that she was thinking about Lissi.

Tati turned back to the letter.

"*Tell Theresa that Martin and his mother left the lager just before we did. His father finally sent money for them to emigrate. Martin kept saying they were going to live in India, but his mother said they were going to the Delhi in Canada, where Martin's father works on a tobacco farm. I will write their address at the bottom of the letter for you. Maybe it is not too far from where you are.*"

"I guess my letter to Martin will come back marked *RETURN TO SENDER* too," I said.

"Probably," Tati said, but then he went on. "Here's something for you, Theresa."

"Frau Besselmeyer writes, *Before he left, Martin gave me a message. You know how Martin is. He told me the message three times and made me repeat it so I wouldn't forget, so here it is:* Ask Theresa if the gnome's eye is helping. *I suppose it means something to her.*"

"Gnome's eye?" Mami said. She looked puzzled. So did everybody else. I squirmed at their curiosity, then shrugged as if I didn't know what the message meant. How could I tell them? They would fall off their chairs laughing if they knew I needed a stone because I was afraid to go the bathroom alone.

Twenty-Six

On a hot afternoon in August, Lydia and I sat in the shade of her verandah, watching the ice wagon roll along our street. Every time it stopped, the iceman walked to the back, lifted the tarp that covered his ice, raised his arm and drove his iron pick into the fissures between the blocks. *Crack! Crack! Crack!* Three sharp strikes made chips fly and the blocks separate. He used an enormous pair of tongs to lift a gleaming block, which he hoisted to his shoulder and carried into a house.

When the wagon stopped across from us, the old horse shifted in his traces, swished his tail at a fly and released a gush of pee. It splashed and splattered on the pavement before it snaked its way into the gutter. Any other day we would have screeched and giggled at the sight. We would have wrinkled our noses and said "Eeeew!" at the smell, but on this hot day we didn't feel like moving, so we sat watching drops of melted ice *drip*, *drip*, *drip* into the puddle until the iceman came back. He was already fastening the heavy tarp to the end of his truck when we strolled across the street. He smiled and passed us two fist-sized hunks of ice before he climbed on his wagon, lifted the reins and *clip-clopped* away.

Clutching our freezing morsels, Lydia and I moved back to the verandah and sat, legs crossed, facing each other. We brushed off stray bits of sawdust and sucked noisily while the ice turned our fingers pink.

When my piece was small enough, I popped the whole thing into my mouth. It was so cold it made my teeth ache, but it was too good to take out.

We sat until I saw the Little Man coming down the street. "There's the Little Man," I tried to say, but with my mouth full of ice, it came out, "M-m-mm-m." That made us giggle. And when the ice popped out of my mouth, bounced off my fingers and fell on my thigh, we shrieked with laughter.

"What did you say?" Lydia finally asked.

"I said, *M-m-mm-m*," I repeated, feeling really silly.

"Can you say that in English?"

I pointed up the street. "There's the Little Man," I said, but to my surprise, the Little Man was nowhere in sight. We stood up, and when we did, I didn't feel like laughing anymore, because I saw the Little Man on the sidewalk, his feet in the gutter, his head hanging. The bag he always carried was on the ground, spilling groceries: bread, grapes, two apples, and a package of caramel candies.

"Silly Buzzard," Lydia said. "He's probably drunk."

"He is not," I snapped, annoyed that she always said such mean things about him.

I hurried down the street and bent to pick up the Little Man's belongings. He smiled. "Sarah," he said.

"Theresa," I said. I helped him to his feet, and we walked home together, his bag in my hand, his hand on my shoulder.

Mrs. Sniderman must have seen us coming, because she came out before we reached the porch, and together we helped the Little Man inside and up the stairs.

That evening, when I went upstairs to the bathroom, I heard noises coming from the wall behind the tub. Dull sounds that came as a steady beat. *Thump! Thump! Thump! Thump!* I froze. Was some creature trying to push its way out?

Thumpity-thump. Thumpity-thump. Thumpity-thump. That was my heartbeat drumming along with the wall noises. My hand slid into my pocket, and I clutched the gnome's eye, but it had no magic to take away my fears.

I'll go downstairs, I thought. I'll tell Mami. I'll ask her to come with me. Then I groaned, because I was sure she'd say: "You have more imagination than brains."

Thump! Thump! Thump! Thump! The sounds went on. How could I stay?

I was in the hallway, my hand on the newel post, one foot on the top step, when I realized the noises weren't coming from inside the wall at all. They were coming from the Little Man's room, and with the thumps came soft gargling sounds that flowed together like a song. I swayed. Part of me wanted to run and leave those sounds behind, part of me realized that something was wrong.

"Hello?" I called, hoping Mami wouldn't hear. She'd scold and say, "I told you not to bother the Little Man."

The gargling sounds went on.

"Hello?" I tried again. I looked around. All the doors were closed. Where were all the other tenants?

I walked to the Little Man's door and tapped. More gargling. I turned the knob. The door opened.

Behind it lay shadows, and a strong, sweet smell like rotting fruit that made my nose curl.

Then I saw him, the Little Man, a dark shape slumped on the bed, rocking, his body *bump*, *bump*, *bumping* the wall. I leaned forward, peering into the darkness. It was hard to see with only the thin light from the hallway bulb, but I thought he was holding something the way a mother might hold a baby.

Was it? Yes. It was Lissi. He was holding Lissi! And he was singing to her in his wet, gargling way. It sounded like, "Hush, Sarah, hush. Hush, Sarah, hush."

I stared. Even in this poor light his face looked as gray as the wallpaper paste we used at school. One side looked as if it had fallen. The eyelid drooped so far down that he couldn't possibly see. His mouth hung open, and foamy drool collected in the corner and overflowed, dripping down his chin in long threads that fell and pooled on Lissi's face. I gasped, stepped forward, then back again.

"She...she's mine...," I began, my voice a thin croak.

The Little Man's head lifted. One trembling hand reached out. Was he was trying to grab me? I pulled in my arms, my hands clenched to my chest.

His mouth opened. "Sarah," he croaked, and then something else. What was it he wanted? I didn't understand, and I didn't wait to find out.

Racing from the room, I grabbed at the newel post and whipped around. I took one long step down and then another. My arms flailed against the walls as my legs ran, but my feet no longer touched the stairs. I'll wake up now, I thought as I fell. It's a dream, and I'll wake up before I reach the bottom. But I didn't. I landed with an enormous crash, and before I was able to talk, the hallway was filled with people.

Mrs. Sniderman was *Oy vey*ing. Mami's hand was over her mouth. "I thought it was a bomb," she kept saying. "I thought it was a bomb." The neighbors from the house stuck to ours filled the doorway and peered in at me. Tati was on his knees probing my arm. "I don't think anything's broken," I heard him say.

I pulled my hand free. "St...stop!" I said. I wanted to shout, but the word came out as a squeak. I sucked in one big breath to keep away the tears that threatened, and told them about the Little Man.

There was a lot of noise then. Mami and Mrs. Sniderman hurried up the stairs. I tried to follow, but Tati held me back.

"Call for ambulance," Mrs. Sniderman shouted to one of the neighbors who spoke English. The man left in a hurry.

When the ambulance turned into Kensington Avenue, Tati herded everyone to the sidewalk. A stretcher was lifted from the back, and two men carried it into the house. Neighbors, drawn by the lights and the sirens, gathered and asked anxious questions.

Lydia came to stand beside me. "What happened?" she asked.

"The Little Man," I said. "I think he's really sick."

"The Buzzard?"

"Don't!" I said, the word exploding from my mouth. "Don't call him Buzzard! He's small and old, and he can't help how he looks. And don't call anybody else names either!"

"Well, fine," she said. "You don't have to make a big deal about it." She put her arm around my shoulders, and I wished I hadn't yelled.

"A stroke," Mami said when she came out, and the word was repeated by the people waiting with us.

"Stroke."

"Stroke."

"Stroke."

Tears were flowing down Mami's cheeks as she bent to tell me, "He still has Lissi. He wouldn't let go. I'm sorry. I know how much you want her back, but I didn't have the heart to take her. He seems to need her so badly."

"I know," I said. "He thinks she's Sarah and...and, I don't know...he thinks I'm Sarah too...and...and maybe he's afraid to die alone."

"No one should have to die alone," she said, and she covered her mouth with her fist to hold back her sobs.

When the stretcher was rolled out, Mrs. Sniderman climbed into the ambulance to sit beside the Little Man. Then they were gone.

In the morning only Mrs. Sniderman came back. She brought Lissi in a brown paper bag. "He is gone," she said. "Maybe is good. He has peace now." Then she put her hand on my head. "When he come here, he told me you are like a *mitzvah* for him, a blessing. It was good you could help him."

"I don't know how she had the courage to do it," Mami said. "I'd never have gone into that room by myself."

Even though I was sad that the Little Man was gone, a kind of warm feeling filled my chest. It grew, until I thought I might explode with pride. I wasn't a mouse. I had courage. My mother said so.

But, as I looked, I saw two lines appear on Mami's forehead, between her eyebrows. "From now on," she said, waving her warning finger at me, "don't ever go into another tenant's room!"

I sighed and nodded, pride and happiness oozing away. It was hard to be brave when there were so many rules to follow.

Twenty-Seven

I t was a relief to go back to school. At the end of my
first day, I tried to tell Mami all my news while I
was peeling potatoes. "Guess what? I'm in a different
room with bigger desks, but I have the same teacher.
Miss Lamb! Again! And there's a new girl. Her name
is Ingrid. She doesn't speak English yet, so I let her
copy my work, and at recess I told her lots and lots
of words."

Dorothy was in my class again too, but I didn't
want to talk about her.

"Are those potatoes almost done?" Mami asked.

"Almost."

"Hurry up then."

Annoyed that she was more interested in dinner than my news, I sucked in my bottom lip and stayed silent until the last potato was peeled and all the pots were on the stove. But when she had time to sit down, I started again.

"And do you know, it's almost like some kind of magic happened over the summer, because I understand what Miss Lamb says now. Not everything, but almost everything."

"I hope that means you'll bring home a better report card this year."

Report card? I didn't want to think about report cards. What I told Mami about understanding so much more was true. What I didn't tell her was that no magic had happened to give me the courage to put up my hand. I didn't tell her that I had never once asked or answered a question at school.

For a long time it was because I didn't know the answers. But later, when I thought I knew, I was still afraid to speak in case my words came out wrong.

"Do you remember that boy Roberto?" I asked, changing the subject. "He didn't come back. Dorothy told us his father said school is a waste of time. He said Roberto didn't learn enough, and now he's a busboy in his uncle's restaurant and has to go to work every day. What is a busboy?"

Mami shrugged. "I don't know. Set the table," she said, going back to the stove. "Your father will be home soon."

—◈◉

The next morning I was surprised to see Roberto standing in the boy's yard at school. When he saw me, he smiled and waved. I waved back.

Going to the boy's side was against the rules. There was no fence to separate the boys from the girls, but there was an invisible line that divided the yard. A line we weren't supposed to cross. I looked around for a yard-duty teacher, and when I didn't see one, I walked toward Roberto. He walked toward me too, and we met near the middle.

"Are you coming back after all?" I asked.

"No, I bring my brother." He pointed to one of the small boys running in the yard.

"Dorothy said you have to work now. Is working hard?"

"Is okay." He smiled a small, sad smile. "School is better."

We were still talking when a bell clanged, and we turned to see Sister Mary Ursula striding our way. I hardly knew her, but everybody said that if you did something wrong, she strapped your hands with a piece of leather. "The slugs," the boys called it. I didn't know anybody that got the slugs, but thinking about it was enough to make me shiver. And now Sister Mary Ursula was looking at me.

"Do you know you're in the boy's yard?" she said.

My mouth opened to say "No!" I wanted to say, "It was a mistake." But, for some reason, Oma's face and her flaming hair flashed into my mind. *Tell the truth*, she had said. *Tell the truth.*

"I…I wanted to say hello to Roberto because last year he was in my class and now he can't come to school anymore."

Sister Mary Ursula frowned at Roberto. "You're not coming to school? What are you doing?"

"Working, Sister. In my uncle's restaurante."

"Working! Indeed! How old are you?"

"Thirteen, Sister. Last week."

"Hmph! Why are you here?"

"My little brother," Roberto pointed. "I bring him. He comes to school this year. He gonna learn good. I'm gonna help him."

"You do that," said Sister. "What's your last name, Roberto?"

"Calucci," he said. "Roberto Calucci."

The bell rang. Sister waved Roberto away, and I saw him walk his brother to the boy's door while

I followed Sister's swirling skirts to the girl's. We were almost there when she turned. "Theresa? Your name is Theresa, right?"

"Yes, Sister," I whispered, thinking that now my punishment would come.

"Thank you," she said, and she walked away.

Thank you? I didn't understand. What had I done to be thanked?

⁓✺

The first Friday of school turned out to be a day to remember. First of all, everybody was talking about Marilyn Bell.

"Sixteen years old. She's only sixteen. And she swam across Lake Ontario from the US of A! D'ya know how far that is? That's thirty-two miles!"

"She almost didn't make it. D'ya see the pictures? She was all covered with black gunk, grease or some-thin', and when she came out of the lake, she puked up dirty water."

"My mother'd never let me do something like that. Marilyn coulda drownded."

"Yeah, but she didn't. The guy on the radio said she'll go down in the history books because of it. Wait and see."

I thought about the first time I saw Lake Ontario.

Onkel Johann had said it was smaller than the ocean, but I remembered how big it looked. And Marilyn Bell swam in that water. That was something. For sure, Marilyn was no mouse.

—✳—

Right after our morning prayers, the classroom door opened and Sister Mary Ursula walked in. We all stood up and said, "Good morning, Sister."

"Good morning, boys and girls," she said before she turned to Miss Lamb to say, "I have a student for you."

When she stepped aside, Roberto walked in. He was wearing blue pants and a white T-shirt. His hair was not only combed, it had a straight part on the left side, and it was so shiny it looked wet. Miss Lamb smiled and pointed him to a desk. He still had to sit at the back of the room, but I noticed that he sat straight and tall and he looked happy.

We didn't hear why Roberto came back until we lined up for recess.

"Sister Mary Ursula and another nun, they come to my uncle's restaurante," he said. "They have dinner. Then they talk to my father and my uncle. 'Keep him here, and he will wash dishes forever,' Sister says. 'Send him to school, and he will grow up to run his own restaurant.' So my father, he say yes, and I come back.

Is because of what you tell Sister," Roberto said, looking at me. "She comes because of you."

That made Dorothy snicker, and she pointed her finger of shame at me. "Theresa and Roberto sitting in a tree," she sang softly. But I ignored her. This *is* a day to remember, I thought. I wasn't going to let anything Dorothy might say spoil it.

Twenty-Eight

October turned out to be a rainy month. Day after day we arrived at school cold and damp. The cloakroom smelled like rubber galoshes and wet wool. We were kept indoors for recesses and during lunch, and by the time three-thirty came, we couldn't wait to get out. We shouted and laughed and raced home, ignoring the gray skies, the rain and the sharp winds that warned of the winter to come.

In social studies we learned about explorers: Prince Henry the Navigator, Bartholomew Diaz and Vasco da Gama. Men of courage, Miss Lamb called them.

One day she printed the word *COURAGE* on the blackboard. "What does it mean?" she asked.

"It's like having bravery," someone said, and she wrote the word *BRAVE* on the board.

"Courage is if you're not afraid, ever," somebody else said. Miss Lamb wrote *UNAFRAID* and turned back to the class.

"Courage is like when you are helping a friend," Roberto said.

"That's right!" Miss Lamb said happily, "Courage *is* helping a friend."

She wrote *HELPING A FRIEND* on the board. That made Dorothy snicker, but she stopped when Miss Lamb frowned at her.

"It's when you've got the guts to do something hard," said George. His words made everybody giggle, and Miss Lamb frowned again, but she didn't say that George was wrong.

"Well, let's talk about courage for a moment," Miss Lamb said. "Do you all agree that the explorers were courageous?" Everybody nodded.

"Do you think they were ever afraid?" The class was silent. She waited. Eventually some people nodded.

"What do you think might have frightened them?" she asked, and because she was talking about something that had been on my mind a lot, I raised my hand.

Miss Lamb's eyes opened wide, and she came over to stand in front of me. "Yes?" she said, leaning toward me.

"Rats," I said. "Probably they were afraid about rats on their ship." What I meant to say was that they were afraid the rats might leave their ship, but Miss Lamb said "Yes!" so quickly that I began to wonder if Martin had his information wrong.

Other hands went up, and more answers were added to the list. Sea monsters. Storms. Getting lost. Drowning. The answers came so fast I couldn't tell who gave them.

I took a breath and raised my hand again. "Having no water," I said.

I could hear Dorothy snort. "They're on the ocean," she said.

"Yes," Miss Lamb said, "they are on the ocean, but they could still run out of water. Why?"

Thanks to Martin, I knew the answer to that question too.

Miss Lamb went on to talk about how dangerous life at sea could be, and I heard her say, "Sometimes sailors were superstitious."

The word *superstitious* caught my attention. It was a new word for me, and I liked its slippery sound. When she explained its meaning, I listened.

And then she asked, "What might a sailor carry to make himself feel safe?"

She wrote a whole list of things on the board: a coin, a picture, a lock of hair, a necklace, a ring, a rosary.

"A stone?" I offered, and I was relieved that Miss Lamb added my word to her list, because I couldn't help thinking that maybe carrying a lucky stone wasn't such an unusual thing to do.

"Can people be afraid and still be courageous?" she asked next.

Around me, kids began to nod.

"Well then," she went on, "can we say that courage is doing the things you have to do even when you're afraid?"

Another new thought…even when you're afraid…

At the end of the lesson, Miss Lamb said, "Your homework is to write about courage. Think about times when you, or someone you know, has shown courage, and write about that."

I thought for a long time before I wrote my paragraph. It was hard to explain my ideas in English, and when I was done, I worried that maybe what I had written wasn't good enough.

The next day Miss Lamb asked us to stand up and read our work. A heavy weight moved in to sit on my chest. It was one thing to answer a question, but to read out loud…to the whole class…in English? I kept my head down, hoping she wouldn't call my name.

"George," she called. I sighed in relief. My ears filled with the sound of my heart beating, *SHWOOM! SHWOOM! SHWOOM!* It was so loud I didn't hear what George said, and the whole time I sat slumped in my chair, my fingers creasing the corner of my page into accordion folds. Outside, rain washed over the windowpanes, and with all that water falling down, I had a sudden need to go to the bathroom. I put up my hand.

"Theresa!" Miss Lamb said. I was surprised at how happy she sounded. "I'm so pleased you volunteered," she said.

I stared. Volunteered?

"But, I…," I began.

"Please, stand up and read what you wrote," said Miss Lamb, nodding her encouragement.

I slid out of my chair and locked my knees to keep them from wobbling.

"Read your work, Theresa," she prodded.

What could I do? I flattened my page and began.

Courage
You have courage if you swimming all the way over a big lake. It is courage to killing a rat. You must have courage to turn on a stove that goes pop. *It is big courage to go to a new country when you cannot talk and understand. And you have courage when you must speak the truth. It is hard to be courage when you are small.*

As soon as I said the last word, I collapsed into my seat, sipping thin mouthfuls of air. I thought I heard Dorothy's annoying snicker, but my heart was beating so loudly I wasn't sure.

"Theresa," Miss Lamb said. Had she called my name before? I looked up. She was looking at me. "You can add something else to your paragraph," she said. "You can add, 'Courage is standing up to read your work in class.'" And she smiled again. This time I smiled back.

Twenty-Nine

"Is that your mother's?" Dorothy asked with a loud hoot as we put on our coats to go home.

I turned my back to her so that she wouldn't see the hot flush creep over my face as I buttoned my raincoat. It did belong to my mother. It was gray and way too big. Even when I stretched my arms, the sleeves dangled over my fingers and the bottom swept the floor as I walked. I pulled up the hood and hid inside.

In the morning I had wailed and stamped my foot in frustration when Mami insisted I wear it.

"It's your raincoat. You wear it," I snapped, the words slipping out before I realized how they would sound.

"That's enough!" Mami had warned, her face dark, her hand up and threatening. She made me put on the horrid thing, and I stayed mad all the way to school.

There were rules about going into the school before the bell, but when I reached the schoolyard, it was empty and the lights streaming from our class-room window looked inviting. I stripped off the offending raincoat and went inside. The hallway was empty, and when I peeked into the classroom, Miss Lamb was working at her desk.

"Good morning, Theresa," she said when she saw me. "Why don't you hang that up?" She gestured toward the raincoat, now dripping a puddle on the hardwood floor. "You can help me hand out papers."

⌁∬◉

It rained on and off most of the day.

"I can wash the boards," I offered at three-thirty, hoping Miss Lamb would let me stay until everyone else was gone.

She shook her head. "Not today," she said. Then she raised her voice so the rest of the class could hear. "Today I want everyone out on time," she said. "It's probably nothing to worry about, but it's raining pretty hard, and I want all of you to go straight home."

That's why I was standing in the cloakroom, dressed in my raincoat, looking like a tent with legs. As I bent to pull on my brown galoshes, Miss Lamb's warm hand gripped my shoulder. "You must be happy to have this today," she said. "It will keep you dry in this drenching rain if anything will."

I glanced up, grateful. From inside my hooded tunnel I saw Dorothy pull her lips into a tight little *O*, as she always did when she was unhappy. She began opening and closing an umbrella with short, sharp snaps.

"Look what my mother bought at Simpson's," she said as she popped the umbrella open.

I looked. We all did. The umbrella was beautiful. It was pink with ruffles around the edges. Little black poodles danced a circle around the top.

"It's certainly elegant," Miss Lamb said, making Dorothy beam.

"But that's bad luck," George said.

"What is?" Dorothy demanded.

"Opening your umbrella inside."

"Is not! It's not! Is it?" Dorothy asked.

"It's a superstition," Miss Lamb said. Dorothy made a face, but she closed the umbrella and put on her coat and boots.

I was still struggling to fit my feet into my galoshes when the classroom lights flashed off. Dorothy and a few of the girls screeched. Miss Lamb told them to stop being silly. Then the lights flashed back on, and she walked us to the doors. "Be careful on your way," she called as we headed out.

At the door Dorothy tried to open her umbrella. She held the handle but couldn't slide the little toggle up. When it finally opened, the wind slipped underneath the cloth and snapped the spokes up and over so the black poodles had their feet in the air, and Dorothy had to dance back and forth to keep the umbrella from blowing away.

Maybe opening an umbrella inside is bad luck, I thought as I hurried across the yard.

Lydia ran up beside me before I reached the gate, and we started for home together.

Sometimes walking in the rain can be fun, but it wasn't fun that day. The rain came down hard and heavy. It danced across the pavement in waves, first one way, then another. For a while the wind came from behind and pushed us. We giggled nervously as we leaned back and let it shove us along, but just when we got used to that, it changed directions and whipped into our faces. When we turned to walk backward, it shifted again. In the gutters the water streamed by, racing toward the sewer grates, where it formed swirling whirlpools or collected into pond-sized puddles.

By the time we reached Spadina Avenue, the sky, which had been gray all day, turned black. The streetlights flashed off and, this time, they didn't come back on, and the street we knew so well turned into a dark tunnel. I was relieved when Lydia grabbed my hand.

"Run!" I shouted, and we ran, hand in hand, struggling against the rain until we reached our street, where we squeezed into the thin shelter of a doorway.

There was nothing welcoming about Kensington Avenue. Trees were bending low in the wind, their branches sweeping the ground, then rising and whipping the air before they bent again in a crazy dance. Empty fruit baskets bounced along the ground, then rose and sailed like kites. Garbage tumbled down the middle of the street or floated in the water that streamed along the gutters.

A brilliant flash of lightning lit the sky. That first flash was followed by another, and then another, and then so many I lost count. Thunder cracked and rang and crashed, the noise bouncing between buildings, hitting our bodies with waves of sound. I was so busy watching, I didn't notice at first that Lydia had dropped to her knees and curled up like a turtle.

"Lydia!" I shouted. She didn't move. I knelt and put my mouth to her ear. "Take my hand," I said. "Take my hand."

I tugged until she rose, and we went on again, staggering up the dark street together.

She stayed beside me all the way to our porch. When I turned the knob, the front door whipped out of my hand and crashed against the wall. It felt like the wind blew us in too. With my legs tangled in Mami's raincoat I couldn't get up, so I stayed on my knees and shoved with all my might to close the door against the storm.

It was then that I heard Lydia's high, keening cry. Outside it had matched the wail of the wind, now it seemed as if that wind had followed us in.

I expected Mrs. Sniderman to scold us for the noise and for the rain and the leaves we had carried in, but her door stayed closed.

Friday, I remembered. Mrs. Sniderman always went out on Fridays. The house was dark and empty. We were alone.

For a moment I didn't know what to do. I remembered all the times Mami said, "Don't bring anyone into the house." But Lydia was crying. Her face was blue-white, and she shook so hard that her teeth clacked. How could I leave her? I unlocked our door and dragged her in behind me.

Inside, I helped her pull off her sopping clothes and gave her my flannel nightgown. Then I urged her toward the davenport and dragged the duvet off my parents' bed to cover her. By that time my own teeth were chattering. I stripped off my clothes and put on dry ones, and we pulled up our feet and huddled together under the duvet's feathery protection.

"Shhhhhhh," I whispered, but I was so scared and so cold that the sound came out, "Sh-sh-sh-sh-sh-sh-sh."

Outside, the wind howled. Rain drummed the windows. In the darkness, the house creaked, rattled, groaned and shook. Lydia kept crying. There was only one thing I could think of that might help.

I made her get up so I could pull the gnome's eye from my treasure box inside the davenport. "Here," I said. "It's good to hold when you're afraid." And we sat again, side by side, our hands around Martin's stone.

After a while we stopped shivering, and Lydia stopped crying.

"I can make up a story about lightning and thunder," I whispered. "Do you want me to?" When she didn't answer, I started.

"Once there were three enormous giants that lived in a big stone castle way up in the sky. There was a mother and a father and a baby giant. Even the baby giant was big. He was so big that an ordinary house would break into toothpicks if he stepped on it."

I glanced at Lydia. She had her eyes closed, and I couldn't tell if she liked the story or not.

"One day the mother giant fed the baby some spinach. 'It's good for you,' she said. But the baby put his lips together and blew. '*P-p-p-p-p-p-phhhh.*' Spinach sprayed out of his mouth and all over the mother. Her face was splattered with green splotches of spinach, and she had to go and wash it off."

Lydia's head sagged to my shoulder. She snuffled and hiccuped, but she didn't tell me to stop, so I went on.

"When the mother was gone, the baby took his metal spoon and threw it on the floor. It was a giant spoon, so when it hit the stone floor, it made a bright flash of light. That made the baby clap his hands and laugh out loud. His claps made big booming sounds. The baby liked the noise. It made him laugh even more.

"Then the baby giant threw down his bowl. It bounced and made another flash, and so he clapped his hands together and laughed loud, loud, loud, and that made lots of booming sounds.

"On Earth, the people saw the flashes and heard the booming sounds, and they called them lightning and thunder."

"That's silly," Lydia said, but when a new bolt of lightning brightened the room, she didn't cry.

Staring out of our feathery cocoon, I sat for a long time before I realized that even though the bedroom was dark and each piece of furniture was

a gray shadow, they were shadows I recognized. There
was nothing new or different in this dark world; no
ghosts or witches or monsters reached out for us. It
was dark, but this familiar darkness was comforting
compared to what was going on outside.

We must have slept for a while, because we both
jumped and gasped as the outside door crashed open.

"Theresa! Theresa!" Tati's voice called.

"We're here," I called as I hurried to unlock our
door.

Tati walked in and swept me up and hugged me
tight. "You're safe," he said. "You're safe. I was so
worried."

Mami repeated those words when she arrived, and
a little while later, so did Onkel Johann.

"I had to come," he told us. "I was so worried.
I wanted to make sure you were all safe."

All that worry told me how big this storm really
was. Because never before had everybody worried at
the same time.

Mami searched our cupboards for a candle. She
found one small stub, but even its tiny light was a
comfort in our dark rooms.

When the power came on again, Onkel Johann
went across the street to tell Lydia's landlady where
Lydia was, so her mother would know where to find
her when she came home. And that's how everybody

ended up in our rooms on the night Hurricane Hazel roared through Toronto.

They all had stories to share.

Lydia's mother told her story while she was sitting on our davenport, a cup of tea in one hand, her arm around Lydia.

"I went to work early because of the rain," she began. "I thought the streetcar might be slow, and I didn't want to be late.

"The elevator was working when I went up to clean the offices. Then the power went off. I waited and waited, but everything stayed dark. Outside, I saw the lightning flashing...flashing over the city... and the thunder...so loud. So loud. I worried about Lydia. I knew she'd be afraid, so I decided to go home. I had to walk down all those stairs, feeling my way in the dark."

She sipped from the cup she was holding, before she said something that made me sit up.

"I...I was really scared," she said, "but there were other people on the stairs, and we kept talking. It helped...hearing voices, knowing I wasn't alone.

"And you," she said, turning toward me. "Lydia has been telling me how you took care of her."

I felt my face flush, but I couldn't help feeling pleased, especially when Lydia said, "Theresa told a story. She has the best imagination of anybody."

When Onkel Johann translated, Mami made a funny face. "More imagination than brains," she said.

But Onkel Johann shook his head. "Do you know," he said, "Albert Einstein believes that imagination is more important than knowledge."

Mami's eyebrows rose, and I thought she looked surprised…pleased even.

"There's great power in stories," he went on, looking at me. "So it's good if you keep telling them."

Mami groaned when she heard, but I sat up straighter.

Then the talk turned back to the storm, and Tati told about walking home from work. "The water was almost up to my knees, and I had to wade all the way up Spadina Avenue," he said. "People had their pants rolled up. Some of them were barefoot, carrying their shoes to protect them from the water, as if that did any good."

"You were lucky," Mami chimed in. "I saw a woman step off the sidewalk. She must have stepped into a hole or something, because she fell, and the water was coming so fast that she was washed down the street. She was screaming. I was screaming. Some men came, and we helped her back to her feet. Imagine. She could have drowned in the street."

The stories went on and on. I listened, hearing time and again how the grown-ups had been afraid of the same things that had frightened me.

I thought about the gnome's eye and how it had given us the courage to face the storm. Martin's river stone. A stone that had no magic at all. Or did it? Maybe the magic in the gnome's eye was like the magic needed to learn English: it only worked when you helped it along.

⁓🙶◎

Dear Martin:

We got your letter. What is it like on a tobacco farm? Onkel Johann said it is hard work to cut tobacco. Do you have to go to work in the fields with the grown-ups?

Tati and I looked for Delhi on the map of Canada, but we didn't find it, and then Onkel Johann showed us where it is on the Ontario map. I'm glad it's not so far away. At least it's not the Delhi in India. Onkel Johann says he will borrow the truck from his store and will drive us to visit you.

I don't have the gnome's eye anymore. I gave it away. There was a man who lived upstairs in our house, and he was mostly nice to me, but he got sick. An ambulance came and took him to a hospital, but then he died anyway.

Last week, Mrs. Sniderman took me to his cemetery, and she put a stone on his grave. She said Jewish people do that. So I put the gnome's eye on his grave. It was the only stone I had, and I thought it would be good if he had something to protect him from all things evil.

Tati still calls me Mouse, even though I'm not afraid as much as I used to be. He says only a fool is never afraid. I guess being afraid is better than being a fool. (Ha. Ha.)

Your friend,
Theresa

Acknowledgments

The Gnome's Eye was written with the help of:

Peter Carver and many of Toronto's storytellers, who encouraged me to research and tell the tales of my childhood;

Barbara Greenwood's writing course;

All the wise and wonderful people in Peter's Thursday-night group and in Hadley Dyer's writing classes who made invaluable suggestions;

The people at Diaspora Dialogues;

Joe Kertes, who mentored me when my book was only a short story;

My first readers: Cheryl Rainfield, Maureen Paxton, Connie Hubbarde, Susanne Farrow and Dan Yashinsky;

My wise and patient editor, Sarah Harvey, and all the other amazing people at Orca;

My family and friends, who support me and celebrate with me.

ANNA KERZ is a retired teacher who immigrated to Canada as a child in the 1950s. In addition to writing for children, she works as a storyteller, telling tales to audiences of all ages. Her first novel was *The Mealworm Diaries*. She lives in Scarborough, Ontario.